PERIL IN PARADISE

Nancy and George went to the lobby of the Grand Hawaiian Hotel to rent a Jeep. After the attendant had given them the keys, they headed for the parking garage.

"It's really quiet down here," George said as they reached the bottom of the escalator and turned left toward the rental car area.

"I think this is it," Nancy said when they reached the F section. She matched the number on the rear bumper of a shiny new black Jeep to the one on the key ring she was holding.

As she went around to the driver's side, Nancy's heart leapt into her throat. The keys fell from her hand and clattered onto the concrete.

Lying facedown on the ground was the body of a man, his arms spread out and a puddle of blood under his midsection. Nancy drew her breath in sharply. On the back of his expensive-looking black suit jacket were six distinct bullet holes!

Nancy Drew & Hardy Boys SuperMysteries

Available from ARCHWAY Paperbacks

A NANCY DREW and HARDY BOYS

SUPER·MYSTERY™

TROPIC OF FEAR

Carolyn Keene

AN ARCHWAY PAPERBACK
Published by POCKET BOOKS
New York   London   Toronto   Sydney   Tokyo   Singapore

This book is a work of fiction. Names, characters, places and incidents are either products of the author's imagination or are used fictitiously. Any resemblance to actual events or locales or persons, living or dead, is entirely coincidental.

AN ARCHWAY PAPERBACK *Original*

An Archway Paperback published by
POCKET BOOKS, a division of Simon & Schuster Inc.
1230 Avenue of the Americas, New York, NY 10020

ISBN: 0-671-73126-2

First Archway Paperback printing November 1992

10 9 8 7 6 5 4 3 2 1

Cover art by Frank Morris

Printed in the U.S.A.

IL 6+

TROPIC OF FEAR

Chapter

One

Joe Hardy saw the giant wave start to form, swelling up against the heavy ocean water and rolling toward the shore. It was going to be big when it broke.

Scrambling onto his neon orange surfboard, he paddled out to meet it. "Let's go, baby, I'm ready," he shouted, adjusting his goggles. Crouching for better balance, he met the wave exactly right and rode just inside the curl.

"Ye-es!" Joe yelled during that magic time when he and the wave were one. They rushed toward shore and Joe let out a laugh of exhilaration. Surfing was great!

In a minute salty water sprayed his face as the cap of the wave came curling over him. His view blurred, and his board shot out from under him. Then the wave slammed down on him, pushing him underwater. When he surfaced, he gulped air with a sense of relief. Joe clutched his board floating nearby and pulled it toward shore, where a small group of onlookers applauded.

"Nice work, Wipeout!" called a girl of awesome beauty wearing a neon blue bikini that perfectly matched her doe-shaped eyes. Her long, straight dark hair hung over her tan shoulders.

"Thanks, Heather," Joe said, shaking back his wet hair and wiping water off his chest with his hand. For a girl who said she wanted to be a model, Heather Farwell seemed to have a lot of free time to spend on the beach, he thought.

"Hey, not bad," added a sarcastic male voice moving up behind Heather. "But what are you going to do when the *real* surf comes up? Think you can handle it?"

Joe squinted against the bright Hawaiian sun and picked out Willy Brannigan standing next to Heather with his worn gray surfboard.

Willy had blond hair and was Joe's height, six feet, but the similarities ended there. Willy was a real put-down artist and impressed with things like designer shades and trendy surf wear. As far as Joe was concerned, Brannigan was a jerk.

"I can handle anything you can," Joe shot back confidently, though he doubted it was true. Willy was a pro, and that last wave was the biggest Joe had ever ridden.

"Well," Willy drawled, "watch me when I'm out there, Wipeout. You might learn something."

Entering the All-Island Surfing Competition under the name Roger "Wipeout" Keenan had been Joe's idea. He and his brother, Frank, had flown to Hawaii two days earlier at the request of Christopher Watanabe, the head of Hawaii's Department of Cultural Affairs and a longtime friend of their father's. Mr. Watanabe had asked the Hardys to help track down a ring of thieves who'd been stealing native Hawaiian art and artifacts.

Willy Brannigan—beach bum, surfer, and party animal—was a prime suspect. So was Heather Farwell, Joe reminded himself, giving her a nod before heading across the beach to where Frank lay on a beach blanket.

"Your manager wasn't even watching, by the way," Willy said with a sharp laugh. "I don't think you have much chance at a prize this week, Keenan."

Joe shrugged. He didn't say anything about the fact that the prize money would barely cover the cost of a trip to Hawaii. As far as he could tell, Willy and the others were risking their necks for new surf gear and their pictures in the paper.

Farther up the beach Joe's brown-haired brother was lying on his stomach, resting on his elbows, a book on Hawaiian wildlife open in front of him. "Looking good, Wipeout," Frank said. "I see Heather was impressed."

"That won't help us nail any thieves," Joe said with a shrug, plopping down next to Frank.

"Hey, you got sand on my book," Frank said, shaking out the pages.

"What's Harry been up to?" Joe asked, nodding to where a tough-looking man with short dark hair sat under a palm tree sipping a cold drink. Harry Leong, the bouncer at one of Waikiki's hippest beach clubs, Surf Riders, was Heather Farwell's boyfriend—and the third suspect in the case.

According to Mr. Watanabe, Heather and Harry were too interested in art for a bouncer and a would-be model. So far, three museums had been robbed right after their visits.

Willy had never been spotted near any cultural institution. But other than that and his actual surfing time, he, Heather and Harry, were always together.

"Something's up," Frank said. "Harry's been busy on the phone."

Joe looked up just as Heather was passing by on her way across the beach to Harry. She gave Joe a little wink and a smile.

"I'm telling you, Joe," Frank said as the brothers watched her retreating figure. "She's got a thing for you."

"So what's this about phone calls?" Joe asked, ignoring Frank's comment as he watched Heather slide onto a blue beach towel.

"He's made two trips to the phone so far," Frank said, nodding in Leong's direction. The beach concession, with its cold drinks, snacks, and telephones, was only a short distance away. Behind it was the parking lot, then the coast road. Beyond the road Joe could see spectacular, jungle-clad mountains towering over the palms.

"Think they're planning another job?" Joe asked.

"Mr. Watanabe said it's been every week for the past three weeks," Frank answered. "By that schedule they should be due."

"But with so many robberies under their belts," Joe said, "what's left?"

"Right here on the island of Oahu there's a lot of treasure, Joe," Frank said. "Not just public museums, but also private ones."

Joe watched Harry Leong whisper in Heather's ear, then jog off to a phone again.

"Hey, Joe, why don't you check in with Cultural Affairs? Maybe you'll be able to hear something Harry says while you're there."

"Okay," Joe retorted with a grin. "And what'll you do? Read?"

"Me?" Frank said. "Oh, I'll just keep an eye on Heather."

"I bet you will," Joe said, fishing change out of his shorts. "Some brother. Keeps the good jobs for himself. Don't forget you already have a girlfriend, Frank. Her name is Callie, remember?"

Frank nodded but continued staring at Heather. "Heather has too much class to be hanging around with those guys," he said.

The brothers continued watching as Heather drizzled sunscreen onto a well-shaped, slender leg. "Looks, she's definitely got," Joe said. "Class? I'm not so sure. Anyway, I'm going to make that call."

Joe chose a phone three away from Harry's. The hulking bouncer was deep in discussion. As Joe picked up his phone, he heard Harry say, "We're coming in for final instructions. Make sure the big man—" He stopped, eyeing Joe suspiciously.

Joe grinned at Harry and proceeded to drop some change into his phone. When Harry turned back to his call, he lowered his voice.

"Hello. Department of Cultural Affairs," came a pleasant voice on the other end of Joe's line.

"Mr. Watanabe, please. It's, uh, Roger Keenan calling." Seconds later Chris Watanabe picked up the phone.

"Hi there, Joe," he said. "Any luck?"

"We may be onto something," Joe said, as Harry hung up and headed back toward Heather. "Have you got that map we asked for? The one that shows the locations of all the major collections?"

"It's waiting for you at your hotel," Watanabe said.

"Great." Joe glanced over at the water, where a surfer was being swallowed whole by a monstrous wave. The "real surf" that Brannigan had talked about must have arrived. As he watched, it occurred to Joe that he could fit his entire knowledge of surfing into a bottle of suntan lotion. Still, if that clown Brannigan could handle it, he supposed he could, too.

"When will you check in again, Joe?" Watanabe asked, interrupting Joe's thoughts.

"We'll call you at home tonight—if we have anything new to report," Joe said. After hanging up, he trotted back to Frank.

"They're leaving," Frank told Joe. "I don't understand—she just put on sunscreen. Something must be up." Joe glanced furtively over and saw Heather and Harry shaking the sand off their beach towels. Then she opened her purse and tossed him a key ring. "I'm going to tail them. Think you can get a lift back to the hotel with someone?"

"Sure," Joe said. "But you're going to miss me in my surfing contest. Some manager you are," he added with a wink.

"Good luck, Wipeout," Frank said, shoving his book into his navy duffel bag. "See you later."

"Hey, Wipeout!" Joe whipped his head around and saw Willy Brannigan waving at him. Behind Willy an official with a clipboard was waving, too. "It's your turn. Didn't you hear them call you?" Willy said.

"I'll be right there," Joe said, trying to sound nonchalant as he slid on his goggles.

Joe saluted the three judges who stood at the water's edge. "Ready!" he yelled. He picked up his board and paddled out into the surf until he reached the spot where the waves were starting to build. He saw the one he wanted and moved out to greet it. Clambering onto his board, he caught the wave perfectly. He knew the judges on shore were watching intently as he rode the crest of the wave.

Then, without warning, his left foot slipped out from under him, throwing him dangerously off balance. Before he knew it, the water was crashing over him, sending him under the surf.

As Joe rolled out of control, his shoulder collided with a rock on the bottom, making him tumble over himself and wince in pain. He scrambled frantically for the surface, but the ocean was a powerful competitor. It seemed a year before his head finally bobbed out of the water.

Joe gulped in air, throwing his head back. What he saw above him didn't comfort him a bit. His board was hurtling down from the sky, aimed right at his head!

Chapter

Two

Frank waited until Harry had started his souped-up red Firebird and screeched onto the coast road. Heather's little car belched blue smoke from its exhaust. "Get a tune-up!" Frank said under his breath as he revved his rented convertible to take off after them.

When the Firebird turned onto the Pali Highway, Frank let a blue Dodge get between Harry and him.

Covered by the Dodge, Frank followed the Firebird through the Pali tunnel, heading toward Honolulu. He lost the car briefly in Waikiki, the heart of downtown Honolulu. Fortunately, a whiff of noxious fumes alerted Frank and he turned his head in time to see Harry's car pull into the entry drive of the Grand Hawaiian Hotel, where Harry and Heather lived. He waited a few seconds before driving after them down the ramp into the underground parking garage.

How did a goon like Harry get to live at the Grand Hawaiian? Frank wondered. The Grand Hawaiian was the oldest, most gracious hotel on Waikiki Beach's famous strip of hotels. Parking where he hoped they couldn't see him, Frank leapt from his car and raced to the escalator. He wanted to arrive in the lobby before Harry and Heather in case they weren't just going to their rooms.

The high-ceilinged lobby was built in the traditional Hawaiian lanai, or veranda, style. It was open on two sides, so balmy breezes could drift through at all times from the hotel courtyard or the Pacific Ocean, a couple of hundred yards away.

At the main desk about a dozen tourists were checking in, most of them silver-haired senior citizens. Frank noticed a number of men in suits filtering through the lobby, too. They appeared to be out of place among the other visitors, who wore brightly colored Hawaiian shirts and casual dress.

Choosing a spot next to a pink marble pillar, where he could observe but not be observed, Frank watched the escalator. Harry and Heather emerged shortly. Great, Frank thought.

Stepping out from his hiding spot, he tried to

weave a path through the people checking in. "Excuse me," he said, nearly colliding with a porter loaded down with luggage.

"Oh, these flowers are exquisite," an elderly woman said loudly. She held the flower lei around her neck up to her nose. At the same time she stepped awkwardly and came down hard on Frank's instep.

"Oh, my! I'm so sorry, dear," the woman apologized. "Are you okay?"

"No problem," Frank said through gritted teeth. He gave her a hurried nod and a smile.

"Wait a minute—you look like my great-grandson, Marc—just like him! He was the one who told me I would love Hawaii, and he was so right." The woman took hold of Frank's arm and gushed, "Isn't it wonderful here? I just love Honolulu and all of Oahu! But the other islands are marvelous, too."

Frank looked over at the elevators. Heather and Harry were still standing there, waiting.

"Oahu, Maui, Kauai, the Big Island, Molokai —every island has a charm all its own," the woman went on. "My niece and I just came back from Lanai and—"

"Aunt Ethel, there you are!" A heavyset middle-aged woman in a loose-fitting muumuu walked up to the old lady. She smiled at Frank and took her aunt's arm. "Who is this young man you're talking to?"

"Doesn't he look like Marc?" the older woman asked the other.

"Ladies, I really have to run," Frank said, walking backward toward the elevator.

The elevator door opened, and Frank turned quickly and smashed into a girl coming out. The girl's reddish blond hair flew out in front of her face as she stepped backward with a surprised yell. "Sorry!" Frank gasped, reaching out to steady her. The girl tilted her face up to him, her eyes widening with surprise.

"I can't believe it!" Frank exclaimed, gazing into blue eyes he would know anywhere. "Nancy Drew!"

"Frank Hardy!" Nancy said, smiling broadly. "What in the world—?"

"I could ask you the same question," he said, giving her a friendly hug. "You look terrific."

"You, too," Nancy said, stepping back to take all of him in. Then, she nodded at the closing elevator doors. "Did you want to go up?"

"Nope. Boy, am I glad to see you," he said, leading her back into the lobby. "I've got a great case to tell you about."

Nancy and her friends had helped Frank and his brother solve more than one case in the past. As far as he was concerned, her input was always welcome.

"Where's Joe?" Nancy asked.

"On the other side of the island, competing in a surfing contest. It's a long story."

"I've got time to hear it. I'm on vacation, believe it or not." Nancy flashed a grin that made

Frank smile. Next to Callie, Nancy was the greatest girl he knew.

"By the way, how's Ned?" he asked casually.

"Oh, he's mad that he couldn't come, but other than that, he's fine," Nancy said. "He's studying super hard, but made me promise to get some sun for him. How's Callie doing?" she asked.

"She's great. Come on, let's go sit outside at the café, and I'll tell you all the details."

The two turned down a columned hallway, and walked past the hotel's specialty shops. Bouquets of flowers hanging in pink arches gave off a heady, lush aroma. Drinking the scent in with a deep breath, Frank felt himself relaxing.

"This really is a kind of paradise, isn't it?" Nancy murmured with a smile.

Frank nodded and took her arm, steering her toward the beachfront café that looked out on the Waikiki surf. Here, on the leeward side of the island, the swells were much tamer. They walked down marble steps from an open veranda to a shaded table and sat in comfortable leather chairs.

"I recommend the lilikoi crush," Nancy told him when the waitress came to the table. "Lilikoi is a native Hawaiian fruit, and it's delicious."

"I'm game," Frank said, smiling up at the waitress. "Make it two lilikois." He turned back to Nancy. "What are you doing in Hawaii?" he asked, breathing in the pleasant tang of the salty breeze.

13

"My dad came for the American Bar Association convention. I'm keeping him company," Nancy said, grinning.

"Good for you!" Frank said.

"Good for Bess and George, too," Nancy said. "They came with us."

"Just for the ride?" Frank teased, and reached out and touched her arm.

Nancy pulled back as if she'd been shocked. "You know, even with number fifteen sunscreen I got a little burn."

Frank looked her over carefully. "Now that you mention it, you are pink."

"I think I'd better stay off the beach tomorrow." Nancy leaned back and eyed Frank intently. "So let's hear it. What's going on?"

"You know Hawaii was once a monarchy, don't you, Nancy?" Frank began, reaching for the lilikoi that the waitress had just put on their table. "Mmmm, this *is* good," he said, taking a sip.

"I've read about the five kings named Kamehameha," Nancy told him.

"Well, that royal family had some incredible artwork and artifacts. Some of it was crafted here, and some was from the Far East. It's displayed in public museums all over the islands because it's supposed to belong to all Hawaiians," Frank went on. "But lately, a lot of it has disappeared. I'm talking about rare treasures—a filigree crown of an Indonesian Prince, a Hawaiian natural pearl vest. Precious treasures."

"What a loss," Nancy said, sighing.

"Anyway, Christopher Watanabe, the head of Cultural Affairs, asked if Joe and I could come see what we could find out. I think he thought of us because the chief suspects are about our age. They hang out at the beach, and one of them is a surfer. That's why Joe is undercover as a surfer, competing as Roger 'Wipeout' Keenan. I'm supposedly his manager."

Nancy broke into a smile. "Wipeout? You're kidding!" She giggled. "Leave it to Joe to come up with a name like that."

"It'll be no joke if they break his cover," Frank said seriously. "These guys are for real. And we think they're about to pull another job."

"They're staying here, at the Grand Hawaiian?" Nancy asked. "My dad knows the owner, Rachel Maxon. Maybe she can help."

"Before you get involved, you should know something about our suspects. They're pretty tough," Frank said. "One's a bouncer, one's a surfer who probably eats rocks for breakfast, and the third one—a girl—is a real sharp cookie."

Nancy gave Frank a crooked smile that told him she was in. "When do I start?"

"How about tonight?" Frank said eagerly. "There's a luau at Surf Riders. It's a club just down the beach about a mile, where the bouncer works. My guess is all three of them will be there, so you can see them for yourself."

"Can Bess and George come, too?" Nancy asked.

"Yeah," said a bouncy female voice behind him. "Can we come?"

Frank turned around to see Bess Marvin and George Fayne grinning down at him. He flashed them a smile.

Bess had on a flamingo pink beach jacket over a bright pink bikini. Her blond hair was tied back in a purple scrunchie. Her cousin George's white terry robe was open, revealing a sleek black racing suit underneath. She was carrying a large willow beach bag.

"Where did you find this guy, Nancy?" Bess asked, touching Frank's shoulder.

"In the lobby," Nancy answered with a smile and a shrug.

"Is this amazing, or what?" George said, brushing a wet lock of dark hair off her forehead. "Is Joe here, too?"

"Yes. Do you want to go to a luau tonight?" Frank asked.

"Are you kidding? That'd be great!" Bess exclaimed. "See, George, I told you we'd find something terrific to do tonight."

"Uh-oh," Nancy said, biting her lip. "I just remembered tonight is the ABA convention banquet. I promised my dad I'd go with him."

"Can't you get out of it, Nancy?" Bess asked, her lively blue eyes pleading.

"I really don't want to get out of it, Bess," Nancy said. "The guest speaker is Ana Saleo."

"I just saw her picture in the paper today," George said. She reached inside her willow beach bag and pulled out a copy of the Honolulu *Sentinel*. On the cover was a picture of a pretty, dark-haired woman giving a speech. The headline read: "Saleo Claims Tanga Is Lying."

"I read that this morning," Frank said. "What's it all about?"

"Rami Tanga was the dictator of the Torquesa Islands," Nancy explained.

"You mean those little islands in the South Pacific?" Bess asked.

"That's right," Nancy went on. "Anyway, about six months ago, the Torquesans finally got fed up with Tanga and had a rebellion that ousted him. That was when Tanga fled to Hawaii, seeking asylum. But according to Ana Saleo, who's a member of the new democratic government, he took the Torquesas' treasury with him. She's trying to get it back."

"I can see why you're excited to hear her," George said. "But maybe you can meet us at the luau after the dinner," she suggested.

"Good idea, George," Nancy agreed, her face brightening. "The banquet starts at six so I should be out of there by ten."

"Joe and I can show Bess and George a good time till you get there." Frank winked at Bess and George.

"Take your time at the banquet, Nan," Bess said, teasing Nancy.

"Hey, there's your father's friend Rachel, the owner of this place." George pointed up to the veranda, where a tall dark-haired woman in an oversized linen blouse and tapered green slacks was approaching the cashier. Her hair was piled on top of her head, and she wore long dangling earrings.

"She's so pretty," Bess said, admiring her. "No wonder your father has a crush on her."

If he does," Nancy said with a shrug. "I can't quite read him when it comes to his romantic life."

"They've known each other awhile, haven't they, Nan?" George asked. "I think I've heard him mention her before."

"Guys," Bess broke in, "I really want to get back to the beach. I have to get some eye exercise looking at all the gorgeous hunks!"

"I'll come, too," George said. "I'd like to do a little more swimming while the sun is still hot."

"See you later," Nancy told them.

Frank found himself watching the attractive hotel owner as she conferred with the cashier. "She looks stressed," he observed.

"With good reason," Nancy explained. "Rachel's parents both died within six months of each other. When she inherited the hotel, she inherited a lot of problems, too. She found out that her dad had taken out a second mortgage, and that he hadn't been paying his taxes. Rachel got hit with a ton of bills all at once. She's barely holding on to the hotel. My dad's trying to help her set up a new payment schedule with her creditors, but it isn't easy."

"I'll bet he saves the day." Carson Drew had a

reputation as one of the best lawyers in the country. "Wait, though—isn't he in criminal law?"

"He's making an exception for Rachel," Nancy said. "He'd like to see her keep the hotel because it's the only privately run one left on Waikiki Beach. All the others have been gobbled up by big corporations."

"Hey! If it isn't Wipeout's manager!"

Frank whipped his head around to see Willy Brannigan staring down at him.

"What are you doing here?" Frank asked.

"The question is what are *you* doing here?" Willy shot back. "It doesn't look very good for you to be sipping drinks with a dynamite redhead while your surfer's in the hospital!"

Frank leapt to his feet. "What? What are you talking about?"

"Yeah, Wipeout's in the hospital, man," Willy said, the grin never leaving his face. "His board came down on his head. Cracked it right open."

Chapter

Three

FRANK STOOD UP and put his face into Willy's. The surfer's smug expression was totally out of place, and Frank felt like busting him in the mouth. "Where is Wipeout?" he demanded, grabbing Willy's orange- and blue-flowered Hawaiian shirt.

"He went to Kailua Hospital about an hour ago," Willy said, putting his hands up in the air. "Hey, ease up! I saved your guy's life. He was out cold when I pulled him out of the water, and his head was bleeding like crazy."

"See you later, Nancy," Frank said, turning his back on Willy. "I'm out of here."

"Not without me, you're not!" Nancy said, tossing some money on the table and taking off after Frank. They hurried down to the parking garage and hopped into his car.

"Why do I go along with Joe's crackpot schemes anyway? He can't surf the waves they have around here!" Frank grimaced as they pulled out of the garage and onto the boulevard. "Man, if anything happens to him, I'll never forgive myself."

"Frank, you're being too hard on yourself," Nancy pointed out. "It's not your fault."

Frank shook his head in frustration and gripped the wheel more tightly. Driving across Oahu toward Kailua Hospital, neither he nor Nancy said another word. When they got to the emergency room, they met the head nurse, a petite woman of about thirty. "Roger Keenan was here," she said. "But we released him. He left by cab about thirty minutes ago."

"You mean he's okay?" Frank asked.

"The wound looked worse than it was. Superficial head injuries tend to bleed a lot," the nurse replied. "He'll be fine."

Nancy went limp with relief, and Frank heaved a sigh. "Looks like we came all the way out here for nothing," he said with a crooked grin.

Riding back to Honolulu, Nancy peered out at the emerald green mountains on one side and the azure ocean on the other. In the distance a rainstorm was hurling itself against the side of a mountain. Above it was a huge double rainbow, the kind Hawaii was famous for.

When they rode past Diamond Head mountain into the Waikiki section of Honolulu, Nancy said, "Drop me at the hotel, okay? I've got to try to get the tangles out of my hair by dinnertime. Convertibles are fun, but messy."

"Here we are," Frank said, pulling up at the Grand Hawaiian. "See you later, Nan. This is really great, running into you and all," he added with a warm smile.

"Well, hunting down art thieves will be fun in this setting," Nancy said as she opened the door and got out. "By the way, where are you staying?"

Frank let out a little laugh. "Would you believe the Economy Inn? When you work for the Department of Cultural Affairs, you go economy all the way. The hotel's not too far from the beach— only nine blocks."

"Poor Frank," Nancy said in mock sympathy. "Tell Joe I'm glad he's okay," she said, stepping back and waving. Frank's convertible pulled away, and Nancy headed into the hotel. She couldn't wait to get started helping the Hardys with their case. Solving a mystery excited her a whole lot more than lying on a beach.

That night at the banquet, Nancy sat with her father as the catering staff cleared the tables for dessert and coffee. "I'm looking forward to meeting these Hardy brothers after all you've told me about them," Carson Drew was saying, "but as a father I hope you're not planning on spending your whole vacation tracking down criminals.

You're not in Hawaii every day, you know, and I'd like to see you just enjoy yourself for once."

"Speaking of enjoyment, what's going on between you and Rachel Maxon?" Nancy knew she was being awfully nosy, but she couldn't contain her curiosity about her dad's situation. He had lost his wife, Nancy's mother, when Nancy was only three. After all these years, she felt he deserved some romance.

"Rachel," Carson began slowly. "Well, I'm fond of her, I'll admit—" He was about to say more when Ana Saleo stepped up to the podium to a burst of applause.

"Thank you," she said, nodding gracefully in response. Ms. Saleo was dark haired and lovely; petite in stature but large with dignity. She seemed slightly shy, but a sharp intelligence and dogged determination shone in her eyes.

"Tonight," she began, "I come to you as the representative of a small nation, the Torquesa Islands. We are a country that has been plundered and betrayed by one man, Rami Tanga. In his twelve years as dictator, he polluted our environment, sold our land to foreign companies, and took all the profits for himself. When the people finally overthrew this tyrant, he fled in the night, taking our treasury with him.

"Now he is living here in Hawaii, under the protection of your government. How will the people of the Torquesas recover the money he has stolen from us? We all know that Tanga has hidden the money well. And we also know that there must be some way that he has access to it. But this money rightfully belongs to the people of the Torquesas, not to Tanga. We must get it back if our fledgling democracy is to survive!"

Her sweet voice had a rising edge to it, one that kept her listeners rapt. "Tonight I'm here to ask for your help. The people of the Torquesas need you to put pressure on your government. In your country the people still have power; your voices are heard. If you speak up for us, we will be heard. Thank you."

"Wow!" Nancy breathed out as the applause died down. "She's dynamite."

"She certainly is," Carson Drew agreed. "But I don't think she'll ever get that money back, Nancy. Tanga's got too many friends in high places."

"Hmm," Nancy said softly. She decided to start reading up on the Tanga affair—maybe she'd think of a way to help.

"No, Nancy, forget it," her father said, grinning. "One case is enough for one vacation."

"You're a mind reader, Dad," Nancy said with a smile. She stood up and gave him a quick pat on the shoulders. "Anyway, I'm off to a luau."

"Don't do anything I wouldn't," Carson called after her.

The luau was in full swing when Nancy's cab pulled up at Surf Riders. She could hear native drums and electric ukeleles strumming as she paid the driver and got out.

Inside waiters bearing huge trays of succulent fruit were heading for the back doors. "Are you here for the luau?" A young hostess, wearing a dozen or so leis around her neck, approached Nancy with a smile.

"Yes, I am," Nancy answered.

The hostess transferred a lei to Nancy's neck. "Come this way," the hostess told her.

They walked through the dining room and across a small dance floor. Beyond it, the restaurant spilled outdoors onto a patio that fronted the beach. From overhead, strands of colored lights shone down on tables filled with immense platters of passion fruit, papaya, pineapple, lilikoi, and more.

A brilliant moon lit up the dancers on the beach. Mixed into the crowd of party goers were native dancers in grass skirts, who were swiveling their hips and gracefully moving their hands to the music. Party goers in cutoffs and shorts did their best to imitate them, some with more success than others. Even the awkward dancers seemed to be having a great time, though.

Nancy saw Frank, George, and Joe, his head wrapped in a bandage covered by a baseball cap, among the dancers. From the energetic thrust Joe was putting into the hula, Nancy thought he must be fully recovered. George not only had a lei around her neck, she was also wearing flowers around her wrists and ankles. She had picked up the hula motions smoothly.

"Hey, there's Nancy!" Frank called, spotting her. Dropping away from the dancers, he walked over to her.

"This is great," Nancy said.

"The food's fantastic, too," Frank agreed. "They cooked it right in the sand, in a big pit. Come on, let's take a walk." When they were on a quieter part of the beach, he confessed, "I haven't made much progress on the case."

"Want to give me a who's who?" Nancy asked.

"Sure," Frank said. "See that stocky guy sitting on a stool by the food table? The one who's facing the dancers?"

"He has to be the bouncer," Nancy said.

"You got it. His name is Harry Leong," Frank told her. "And the girl standing next to him—the one with the long dark hair and short bangs—is Heather Farwell, his girlfriend."

"She's pretty enough to be a model," Nancy said.

"Right," Frank said. "So why is she hanging around with a goon like Harry?"

"Is Willy here?" Nancy asked.

"Yes," Frank said. "But I don't see him now."

"Wait, I think I do," Nancy said in surprise as she scanned the shoreline. "He's with Bess." Then Nancy noticed that Bess was holding hands with the surfer! "Hey, Bess!" Nancy called.

Bess trotted over to Nancy and Frank, pulling

Willy after her. "Nancy!" she cried, "I want you to meet my friend. This is Willy Brannigan. He's a surfer—a real one. He surfs in contests and everything."

"I know. We met earlier today at the Grand Hawaiian," Nancy said. "Hi, Willy."

The surfer grinned at Nancy and Frank, too. "Hey, you two."

"Guess what, you guys," Bess said, bubbling. "Willy wants me to go to Waimea Beach on the north shore tomorrow to watch him surf. Isn't that fantastic?"

"Frank'll be there," Willy said with a smile that was only slightly poisoned. "Right, Frank? He's Wipeout's manager."

"Wipeout? Who's Wipeout?" Bess wanted to know.

"Somebody call me?" Joe called, approaching from the mass of dancers.

Nancy quickly pretended to lose her balance in the sand, so she could grab Bess's arm tightly. The two friends had been through enough together so that Bess got the message. She gave no indication at all that she knew Joe.

"Bess," Frank said coolly, "I'd like you to meet Roger 'Wipeout' Keenan. He's surfing in the competition tomorrow, too."

"Hi, Wipeout," Bess said casually, though Nancy knew she must be dying of curiosity.

"I'd better split," Willy said, turning to Bess. "I want to get a good night's sleep so I'm prepared tomorrow." The wary look in his eyes made Nancy think that sleep was the last thing on his mind. "See you in the morning, Bess?"

Bess grinned and nodded and watched him go with a wave. "He's so-oo cute, isn't he?"

Frank frowned as he saw Willy stop to talk with Heather and Harry. "I hate to tell you this, Bess, but Willy Brannigan may be a thief—an art thief, to be exact."

"Okay, you guys. Out with it. What's going on?"

"We'll fill you in, Bess," Nancy said. "But first I want to get some serious partying in. Now, who's going to show me how to hula?"

The next morning Nancy awoke to find Bess sitting on her bed, painting her toenails. Around her were half a dozen discarded shorts and tops.

"Morning, Nan," Bess chirped. "Wasn't I a genius to pack this mauve nail polish?"

George's head popped up from her pillow. "What's that smell?" she asked, wrinkling her nose.

"Nail polish. I have a date this morning, remember?" Bess said, twisting the cap on. "I can't wait, either. I love surfing contests."

"Don't forget to keep your eyes and ears open, okay?" Nancy said. "And don't blow Joe's cover, whatever you do."

"Don't worry," Bess said. "You know, I've been thinking. I bet Heather and Harry are the real thieves. Willy is probably just their friend.

According to Frank's contact, Willy's never been seen at any museum, and he seems like such a really sweet guy."

"Well, if you hear anything that sounds the least bit suspicious . . ." Nancy warned.

"I know, I know," Bess said, rolling her eyes. "See you at the beach later!"

When she was gone, Nan and George got ready and went down to the lobby to rent a Jeep for the week. "Here are the keys," said the attendant. "It's in space number forty-three F on the lower level. Make a left at the bottom of the escalator."

Nancy stopped to buy a newspaper with a front-page story about Rami Tanga, and Ana Saleo's efforts to find the missing money. Nancy bought a magazine, too, with a photo of Tanga's chauffeur-driven limousine emerging from heavy iron gates. "It says here that Tanga has three residences in Hawaii—one here on Oahu, over-looking Honolulu, one on Maui, and one on the island of Hawaii, the one they call the Big Island. 'He is presently staying in Oahu,'" she read.

George glanced at the picture. "Pretty nice house. Is that him driving?"

"No, that's got to be the chauffeur. Boy, that's a grim face, huh?" Nancy said. "There's Tanga, with his hand up to hide himself from the cameras. I would, too, if I were him. What a rat." Nancy shoved the magazine into her handbag.

They had reached the bottom of the escalator and were turning left to head for the rental car area. "It's really quiet down here," George said.

"I think this is it," Nancy said when they reached the F section. She matched the number on the rear bumper of a shiny new black Jeep to the one on the key ring she was holding.

As she went around to the driver's side, Nancy's heart leapt into her throat. The keys fell from her hand and clattered onto the concrete. There, lying facedown on the ground, was the body of a man, his arms spread out and a puddle of blood pooled under his midsection. On the back of his expensive-looking black suit jacket were six distinct bullet holes!

Chapter

Four

"WHAT'S THE MATTER, NAN?" George asked, moving around from the passenger side. "You look like you've just seen a—aaah!" A small scream erupted from George when she saw the body.

Nancy grabbed her friend and held her tight. "Oh, George!" she whispered.

There was a slight noise not far away—maybe the sound of a shoe scraping on concrete. Nancy tensed and her eyes darted around, searching for the source of the noise. She saw nothing.

"Did you hear that?" Nancy whispered into George's ear. As she spoke, the noise came again, sharper this time. Nancy saw a black-clad figure rise from behind a white sedan about fifty feet away. She saw the flash of light off metal.

"Duck!" she yelled, pushing George down and falling next to her. There was a soft spit from a silencer-muffled gun, and the windshield of the car next to them shattered.

"He's after us!" George whispered, cowering near the dead man.

Nancy could hear feet scraping on the concrete —moving closer and closer. "We'll find a way out, George," she said, wondering if it was true. Peeking under the Jeep, she saw a pair of tan men's shoes approaching.

Then all at once there were loud voices coming their way. A group of people, laughing and talking, had entered the garage. The man in the tan shoes stopped, turned, and quickly ran out, past the people, to the street. "Saved!" Nancy said. George gave a relieved laugh that quickly turned into a choked sob as the two girls helped each other up.

"He has a gun!" one of the people who'd entered the garage said loudly.

"I guess he didn't want to kill us in front of so many witnesses," Nancy said, watching the group of at least twelve stop at a large rental van marked Hanauma Beach. With them was a uniformed employee.

"Did you get a look at the gunman, Nan?" George asked, still a little shaky.

"He had a black stocking over his head and was carrying a black briefcase," Nancy told her.

"Excuse me!" she called to the group, who seemed to be confused and frightened. "Could somebody call the police? There's been a murder."

The people in the tour group began talking at once as the uniformed man ran over to check out the body. Horrified, he dashed off to call the police. The crowd stood still, afraid to come any closer to the body. "A murder!" gasped a silver-haired woman. "Imagine."

Nan bent down to examine the body more closely. There was no doubt the man was dead. She noticed now for the first time that his rear pants pockets were turned inside out. Nancy figured that the gunman must have taken the dead man's wallet.

"Look, Nan," George said, pointing under the Jeep.

Nancy saw a package wrapped in brown paper. A corner of a bright yellow mailing label remained, but the contents had been removed.

Nancy reached under and slid out the package and a bunch of battered, dried yellow flowers. Nancy guessed that they had been inside the package. "It looks to me as if the gunman ripped open the package," she observed, "and finding only flowers, he threw them down."

"But why would he take the time to remove the label?" George wondered.

Nancy shook her head. "This wasn't an ordinary robbery, George. Ordinary robbers don't carry silencers. Poor guy. I wonder who he was."

The corpse was wearing a suit and had a special kind of bracelet attached to his wrist. Nancy had seen them before—her father sometimes used them—the kind that hooked like a handcuff to a briefcase filled with valuables. A courier's bracelet.

Footsteps pounded down the concrete, heading toward the girls. At the same moment a siren wailed into the garage, and the screech of wheels told Nancy the police had arrived—in force.

Three uniformed officers stepped out of the car as two more came from the stairwell. With them was a tan, muscular man in a black golf shirt and beige slacks. "Where are the two girls who discovered the body?" he asked, striding forward.

Nancy put a hand up, and the man walked toward her, holding up a gold badge. "I'm Captain Morita of homicide. What have we here?" he asked, bending down beside her. He didn't wait for an answer. "Miss . . . ?"

"Nancy Drew," Nancy said, giving him a polite nod. "And this is my friend, Georgia Fayne. After we discovered the body, the killer tried to shoot us. He was wearing a stocking over his head and carrying a gun with a silencer in his right hand. A briefcase was shoved under his left arm. When he fired he missed us and hit that windshield."

"We also found this empty package and some sort of dried flowers," George added.

"You'll make excellent witnesses," the captain said. "Are you here on vacation?"

Nancy and George nodded.

"Well, I'm afraid you're going to have to come down to the station house," the officer apologized. "We'll need a statement, and you'll want to file a complaint."

"Glad to help," Nancy said, watching the police photographer snap pictures of the dead man. "Come on, George. Let's get out of here."

"The sooner, the better," George said with a little shiver. "But can I go upstairs to change my clothes really quick?" she asked, pointing at her now-grimy white slacks. The captain nodded and signaled an officer to go with her.

"Weren't George and Nancy going to come out here to Waimea after they picked up their car?" Frank asked Bess as they scanned the water, watching the surf competition. Willy and Joe were both out a ways, waiting for waves to ride.

"Yeah," Bess said. "I wonder what's holding them up. There goes Willy!" she shouted, standing up. Her gauzy white beach cover-up fluttered in the breeze as she raised her arm to shade her eyes. "He's so good."

"Tell me again," Frank said, standing next to her now. "What did Willy talk about on the way out?"

"He just said how neat it was to be a surfer, and how my eyes are as blue as the Pacific," Bess said a little impatiently.

"Dreamy," Frank said flatly. "And he didn't ask anything about me or Joe?"

"Well, sure he did," Bess said with a shrug. "He wanted to know if I knew you. And I told him I'd just met you. Don't worry, Frank. I'm not going to blow your cover. I'm an ace at keeping secrets. Didn't Nan tell you that about me?"

Frank laughed, and Bess joined in. Everyone knew that Bess loved to talk. Keeping secrets was about as natural to her as palm trees on the moon. "Of course, I trust you," Frank said. "But I worry about you hanging around with Willy."

"Oh, stop," Bess chided him. "Look!" she shouted. "There goes Joe—I mean Wipeout."

Frank watched his brother ride the wave, skillfully negotiating it into the shallow water. "Hey, he's looking good out there," Frank said, impressed.

A gust of wind lifted Bess's straw hat from her head. When she turned to retrieve it, she saw Harry Leong hurrying across the beach. "Hey, Frank," Bess said, poking him lightly in the arm. "Where do you think Harry's going? He looks worried."

Frank saw the bouncer trotting over to Heather, who was relaxing under a palm tree. He whispered in her ear, and she sprang up, quickly stuffing her towel in her beach bag. Then she ran for the parking lot, keys dangling from her hand.

"I'm out of here," Frank told Bess. "Keep up the good work, huh?" Following Heather, who made for her Firebird, Frank raced to his convertible. He was two cars behind her as she took the turnoff for Honolulu and poked her head out the window, looking behind her. He followed her all the way into Waikiki, where she stopped at Surf Riders. There she handed her keys to the parking attendant and went inside.

What was she up to? Frank wondered. He checked his watch. It was three-thirty. He'd just tell her he'd stopped by the club for a cold drink. Maybe he could talk to her and get some information out of her.

Seen in the light of day, the restaurant was a dump. What a contrast from the night before, when the colored lights had made everything beautiful.

Sliding into a booth, Frank checked around for Heather. As soon as she emerged from the ladies' room, she spotted Frank.

Her eyes registered momentary surprise. Then she smiled and sidled over to him, sitting down with him.

"You came to see me?" she said in a sultry voice. It was more a statement than a question.

Faced with the truth, Frank thought fast. "Yes, I did," he said, gazing into her ice blue eyes. "I'd like to get to know you better."

"Oh, really? Is that so?" Heather flashed him a smile and leaned close. "That's very friendly of you. What do you want to know?"

"Well, what's with you and Harry? Is it a serious relationship?" Frank asked.

"Sometimes yes—sometimes no," she answered coyly. "Come on, let's dance."

On the dance floor Frank became momentarily lost in her spell.

"You're a good dancer," she said, gazing up at him with a sweet, sincere smile.

"Thanks," he murmured, eyeing the door. He was hoping Harry hadn't made it back yet. Frank didn't think the bouncer would appreciate his dancing ability as much as Heather did.

When the song ended, she took him by the arm. "Let's get something to drink," she suggested. "I'm really thirsty."

"Yeah, I'll have a club soda," Frank said. He watched her walk over to the bar, and order the drinks. Frank decided to hit the men's room.

"Any chance of us getting together tonight?" Frank suggested after he returned to the table.

Heather eyed him cautiously. "Tonight I'm busy," she said. "Maybe tomorrow."

The drinks came. Frank noticed that the day bouncer brought them over. A brief glance passed between him and Heather.

"Funny, I'm not really thirsty," Frank said, pushing away his glass of club soda.

"Drink it," the bouncer ordered. "It'll do you good." The man towered over Frank menacingly.

"Oh, well," Frank said, suddenly feeling uneasy. "Here goes." He took a sip of the soda, but it tasted okay. He took a few more. Clever of me to order club soda, he thought. It's not easy to slip a mickey into plain old—

Whoa. Suddenly Frank felt the world shift.

Was it an earthquake? No, it was no earthquake —it was *him*.

"Let's dance some more," Heather said. Frank started to say no, but the words wouldn't come out. Heather helped him up and guided him around the floor. "So," she said. "What's this big interest in me all of a sudden? Is it because I'm so good looking, or what?"

"Well, actually," Frank heard himself say, "I think you might be involved with—" Wait a minute! What was he saying? "Hey," Frank said, trying hard to get his thoughts together. "What was in that club soda? Did you—?" He was weaving, now. "Well, I'm going to call the—"

He never finished. A huge hand grabbed his arm from behind, and twisted—*hard*.

"Okay, bud," said the big brute. "You've had one too many. Let's see some ID."

Frank felt his wallet being pulled from his back pocket. A few seconds later the bouncer roared, "You're underage, and you're out of here!"

"But I haven't—" Before Frank could get the words out, he felt himself being lifted off the ground, shoved through the door of the club, and thrown to the ground outside. "Ow!" Frank yelled, hurting all over from the impact.

He heard whistles blowing in the distance, and footsteps running toward him along the pavement. He tried to get up but soon realized that his body was no longer obeying his brain's commands. Heather—she was onto him. They were onto him, and onto Joe. He had to warn Joe, before it was too late. . . .

As if in a dream he heard the bouncer saying, "This guy's been making trouble around here all week, officer. He came in here drunk." Frank wanted to object, to tell the police what had happened, but the switches in his brain were all shutting down. The world swayed one last time —and went black.

Chapter

Five

SITTING IN Captain Morita's beige office, Nancy and George shared every detail they could about the shooting incident in the parking garage. The captain leaned back in his swivel chair, absently pulling a rubber band across his fingers as he listened. "I don't like it a bit," he said when they were through. "Especially the part about the silencer. That's heavy for a robbery."

"But, Captain," Nancy said, "if it was just a robbery, why did the killer take the time to remove the label from the package?"

"Maybe he didn't," the captain said with a shrug.

"And then there are those yellow flowers,"

41

Nancy said, biting her lip, trying to figure out how they could be connected.

"Oh, I wouldn't worry about them," the captain said with an impatient laugh.

"Captain Morita," George spoke up, "Nancy's solved lots of cases! She's usually a step ahead of everyone."

Nancy gave George a sharp look, but too late. The captain reacted exactly as Nancy feared.

"Look, girls, for your own safety I don't want either of you involved in this," he warned them. "My department will take care of everything."

"Aren't you even a little curious about those flowers?" Nancy asked. "They might be a clue."

"Not really," the captain answered with a shrug. "But I will have one of my people check them out since they were found at the scene."

Nancy had to bite her tongue. Captain Morita didn't impress her as being particularly astute. He seemed determined to make the murder an open-and-shut case of robbery. Then, too, Nancy realized, murder on Waikiki was not something any official would want publicized. Murder and tourism weren't a good mix.

"My advice to you is simple," Morita told Nancy and George with a weary smile. "Just go and enjoy your vacation. If and when we find the murderer, we'll call you." He led them out into the reception area, where the station door burst open, and two officers came in, dragging a woozy Frank Hardy between them.

"This kid's drunk, Captain. He's underage,

too," one of the officers said. "We found him on the sidewalk. Should we lock him up?"

"Wait!" Nancy cried out. "He's our friend!" She raced over to him. "Frank, are you all right? What happened?"

"Friend of yours, huh?" Captain Morita said dryly, raising an eyebrow in Nancy and George's direction. "All right, sit him down on the bench here for a while."

"I can drive him to his hotel," Nancy suggested.

Morita scrutinized her. "Okay," he finally said. "There's no complaint out against him, is there?" he asked his officers.

"No," one of them answered. "But the bouncer at Surf Riders wasn't happy with him."

"Surf Riders?" George repeated. She and Nancy exchanged glances.

"I was drugged," Frank mumbled suddenly. "They slipped me a . . . mickey. . . ."

"Drugged, huh?" Captain Morita said doubtfully. He leaned forward and took a whiff of Frank's clothes. "Whiskey," he said, wrinkling his nose.

"No," Frank insisted. "They must have poured that on me after . . . drugged . . ."

The captain practically laughed. "And why did they do that? You've still got your wallet, haven't you?"

Frank felt for it and nodded. Yes, it was still there.

"Then why would they slip you a mickey, my

43

friend?" the captain pressed Frank. "Just for laughs?" With that, he let out a laugh of his own. "Take your friend home, girls. Let him sleep it off."

By the time Nancy and George had gotten Frank into their Jeep, he seemed a little more coherent.

"Hey, what are you doing here?" he asked. "You're supposed to be at the beach."

Nancy and George quickly told him what they had found that morning in the parking garage. That seemed to bring Frank around. "Murder?" he said. "In the Grand Hawaiian?"

"The police don't have any leads, either," Nancy said.

"I'll bet *you* do, though," Frank said, managing a half grin.

After Nancy told him about the torn-off label and the yellow flowers, Frank shook his head. "I guess you won't have time to help us with our case now."

"Oh, no, I'm still interested," Nancy said. "As for the murder, other than finding out about the package and the flowers, there isn't much I can do—"

"Wait a minute," George broke in. "What *were* you doing at Surf Riders, Frank?"

"Following Heather," he told them. "I thought I'd talk to her, see what I could find out.

"Anyhow, here's the bad news," he added. "I think our cover's blown. Both mine and Joe's." He frowned, remembering how Heather had looked back at his car. It smelled like a setup to him. "You know, I think she wanted me to follow her and planned to drug me all along."

"To warn you off the case?" Nancy asked.

"Seems odd, huh? But it's the only reason I can figure."

"Here we are." Nancy pulled into the Economy Inn parking lot. They found healthy-looking Joe sitting by the pool in front of the hotel. Nancy filled him in on what had happened as they helped Frank back to the Hardys' room.

"I've got news, too," Joe said as they went inside. "I overheard Harry on the phone again, and get this—he said 'tonight's the night'! He also said they were going to 'island-hop' after that."

"Good work, Joe!" Frank exclaimed. "Now, all we've got to do is figure out where they're going to strike and wait for them."

"Nothing to it," Joe said sarcastically.

"Hey," Frank said, "there aren't that many places on Oahu they haven't already hit." He pulled out a notebook and flipped the pages. "They've already done the Bishop Museum and the Polynesian Cultural Center. . . ."

Joe glanced over Frank's shoulder. "That one looks like a good bet," he said, pointing. "I read that the Royal Mausoleum has a special exhibit of artifacts there now. Stuff that belonged to the royal family."

Frank nodded. "There'd be a lot more to steal there now than at any of the other places left on

our list. What do you say, girls? Are you with
us?"

"Count me in," Nancy said, eager to help.

"Me, too," George said. "And Bess will certainly want to come. She's dying to find out
whether Willy's a crook."

"Well, guys, we'll head back to the Grand
Hawaiian," Nancy said, getting up from the bed.
"Come on, George. Bess will be wondering what
happened to us."

"We'll meet you in your lobby at seven," Frank
told the girls. "Think I'll have a nap till then. I
still feel kind of out of it."

"See you at seven," Nancy said brightly. "Oh,
and feel better, Frank."

Nancy and George ran into Bess arm in arm
with Willy in the lobby of the Grand Hawaiian.
Her slightly sunburnt face was glowing. "Nan!
George! Guess what?" she exclaimed. "Willy
won today! Isn't that fabulous?"

"Fabulous," George echoed, trying to keep the
sarcasm out of her voice. "Nice going, Willy."

"Congratulations," Nancy chimed in.

"Thanks," Willy said with a smile that was
genuine for a change. Funny, Nancy thought, but
around Bess, Willy seemed like a fairly nice
person.

"He's invited me to go on the dinner cruise
that he won today," Bess went on. "You guys are
going to have to do without me somehow." She
wasn't exactly crestfallen, Nancy noticed.

Willy's eyes darted quickly around the hotel, and he stepped back from Bess. "See you at seven, okay?"

"Sure," Bess answered. "I'll come down to the lobby."

With a wink aimed straight at Bess, he turned and strode out of the lobby. "Ciao, ladies," he added as he left.

"Mmmm," Bess sighed, watching Willy saunter off. "He's adorable. And you know what? He can't be the thief you're looking for—he doesn't know the first thing about art."

George rolled her eyes at Nancy, who said, "Come on, Bess. You'd better get ready."

"Tomorrow they're at Makaha Beach if the waves are good," Bess told her friends as they went down the hall to their suite. "I love it! The contest moves to all the best beaches. The surfer winning the most competitions gets a thousand dollars. Hey, how was your day, guys?" Bess added suddenly. "You never showed up at the contest."

"We had a pretty dull day. Except for finding a dead body and getting shot at," Nancy quipped at the door to their room.

"Don't joke like that, Nan," Bess scolded. "You know it gives me the creeps."

"Uh, Bess, to tell you the truth—" Nancy stopped short as she unlocked the door to their room and poked her head in.

"Oh, no," she gasped. "Our room! It's been ransacked!"

Chapter

Six

Nancy, Bess, and George were speechless as they stared at what had once been their neat suite. All their suitcases had been emptied, drawers pulled out and dumped, and the closet stripped.

"Gosh, even I couldn't make a mess like this," Bess murmured, gawking at the room.

Nancy stepped over some bedding and examined a torn pillow at her feet. "Slashed," she announced. "The mattresses, too. Someone was definitely looking for something."

"Um, you guys mentioned something about getting shot at?" Bess said quietly. "Is there more you want to tell me before I pass out?"

Nancy and George quickly filled Bess in on

what had happened down in the parking garage and afterward in the police station.

"Here's my money and your traveler's checks, Bess," said George, who'd been busy searching the floor around the bureau. "Nancy, you had all your money on you, right?"

"Yup," Nancy answered, wandering into the bathroom. "Everything's okay in here." She frowned thoughtfully. "Obviously this was no robbery. Also it can't have been an attempt by the gunman to eliminate us as witnesses because he'd try to kill us, not trash our room."

"Then someone must have been searching for something. But what?" George asked, as baffled as Nancy.

"Good question," Nancy said.

"Well, I know one thing," Bess broke in, "I'm not staying in here another minute. I want to switch to another room—if not another hotel."

"Let's go see Rachel," Nancy suggested. "I can't bother my dad just now—he's tied up all day."

Outside Rachel Maxon's office a few minutes later, Nancy tapped on the half-opened door.

Rachel looked up from an enormous spread of papers on her antique white desk. The window behind her framed a spectacular view of Waikiki Beach. "Hello, girls," she said, standing and moving toward them. "I'm sorry I haven't spoken to you about your experience in the garage this morning. I tried to contact you, but you must have been tied up with the police. Are you all right now?" she asked.

"We're fine," Nancy quickly assured her. "But unfortunately, something else has happened." Rachel said nothing—her mouth opened a little and moved silently up and down once.

"Our room's been ransacked," George said.

"What!" Rachel exclaimed.

"Nothing was taken, but it's a wreck," Bess added. "Is there any chance we can get another suite?"

"Of course! Oh, of course!" Rachel said breathlessly. "I'm so sorry this has happened." She picked up a telephone on her desk. "Renee, is four-twenty-five available? Good. You can transfer the belongings from four-seventeen. Also, ask security to meet me in four-seventeen—immediately." As Rachel hung up the phone, she winced and clutched her stomach.

"Are you all right?" Nancy asked, concerned.

"I'll be f-fine," Rachel managed to say. "I've got a stomach problem—stress brings it on. Lately, I've been under a lot of pressure. And to top it off, now there are several global corporations who want to buy me out and tear down the Grand Hawaiian."

"That would be horrible! It's such an elegant old place!" George said.

"But if they can get rid of me and put a high rise on this land, they'd make a lot more money," Rachel explained. "They're trying to drive me out of business by renting rooms in their hotels for much less."

"But everyone loves the Grand Hawaiian," Nancy pointed out. "Business seems good, too. Maybe their tactics aren't working."

"If that were my only problem, Nancy, I could fight them," Rachel said with a sigh. "But I have other troubles." She explained about the money she owed to the bank and the back taxes to the IRS.

"But how could things have gotten so out of hand?" Bess asked.

Rachel smiled sadly and said, "Apparently, my father had a rare stomach disease that he never told anyone about, not even my mother. His treatments were expensive and not completely covered by insurance. Anyway, now the IRS is determined to collect the money I owe them. You can't believe the things I've had to do, just to stay in business," she said almost to herself.

"Like what?" Nancy asked.

Rachel seemed startled, as if she'd just awakened from a dream. She shook her head and said dismissively, "Oh—all sorts of things. I considered taking out a *third* mortgage. But even the bank advised me to tear down the hotel and build a high rise."

"How could anyone advise you to tear down a beautiful old building?" George said.

"When I was growing up, there were other lovely buildings here on Waikiki, some even more beautiful," Rachel said, remembrance in her eyes. "They were valued for their beauty, but now the only value is profit, profit, profit. In the days before the big corporations, people took care of the land. There was no pollution. Now my beautiful Hawaii is becoming just like every place else.

"Listen to me going on about my problems after what you've been through today. I do apologize. It seems as if I've done nothing but apologize for the past half hour. Well, I won't say I'm sorry again—even though I am."

She scribbled a note and handed it to Nancy. "Please go and have some dinner—on me."

After thanking Rachel, the girls grabbed a quick snack and went to the lobby to wait for Frank and Joe. It was Willy Brannigan who was waiting there for them, instead. "Listen, Bess," he told her, sounding nervous. "I'm sorry about this, but I can't make the dinner cruise tonight. Something's come up."

"Oh, no! What is it?" Bess asked.

Willy became flustered. "Uh, I have to help a friend who's moving," he said. "His landlord threw him out kind of suddenly."

"Can I come? I can help," Bess suggested.

"Uh, he doesn't live in the kind of neighborhood you'd want to be in," Willy said. "Look, I'll see you tomorrow at Makaha, okay? We'll do a cruise another night. I promise."

"Okay, Willy." Bess tried to smile, but it was clear she was terribly disappointed.

"He's not the best liar in the world, is he," George said as they watched Willy leave.

"George, has it ever occurred to you that you may be wrong about Willy?" Bess asked, her voice raised. "Sorry, I'm just disappointed. The dinner cruise sounded so exciting."

Seeing the Hardys come in, Nancy waved. "Hi, guys," she said, greeting them.

"Guess what?" George said. "Somebody broke into our room and tore it apart, looking for something."

"What?" Joe asked.

Frank nodded seriously. "It looks as if we may all be in danger."

Bess blinked. "Even me?"

Frank shrugged. "You're with us, aren't you?" he said.

"I'd probably be safer with Willy Brannigan," Bess said. Nancy wasn't so sure but didn't say anything.

"Well, come on," Frank said, leading them outside. "We'd better head over to the Royal Mausoleum if we want to get there before our friends do."

"Hey, where's Willy tonight?" Joe asked.

Bess frowned. "He canceled," she said, not meeting his eyes. "Something came up."

"Something very vague and very sudden," Nancy said pointedly.

"Well, cheer up, Bess, I have a feeling you might run into Willy tonight after all," Frank said under his breath.

They all piled into the Hardys' convertible. Driving uphill to the edge of town, Nancy turned and gazed out the rear. The orange of the sunset was reflected as a vast golden slick on the ocean's surface.

Bess turned around, too. She saw only the boats pulling out of the nearby marina. "There go the dinner cruise ships," she said wistfully. "And I'm still hungry."

"How can you think of food at a time like this," George said. "We're going to the Royal Mausoleum, where the spirits of old Hawaii walk at night. Oooooo . . ."

"Quit it, George," Bess said, laughing in spite of herself. "I don't need my own cousin scaring me to death."

A few minutes later Frank slowed down and steered off the shoulder of the highway. "Here we are," Frank said. About one hundred feet ahead was the entrance road to the mausoleum. "We'll walk the rest of the way."

They got out of the car and made their way to the deserted entrance of the mausoleum. There was no gate and no security guards visible.

"Look at the size of this place," Frank said, taking in the stately marble buildings set on the wide and open lawn.

"Mr. Watanabe said the budget cuts really hurt security at all the public museums," Joe explained. "He wanted to put on some guards here, but the state couldn't afford it."

Just past the gateway, signs pointed to various nature trails in the forested area around the museum. Frank pulled a brochure out of his pocket and read in the dying light. "According to this map, the trails come out at different points overlooking the mausoleum. I suggest we split up and go to the far ends of the trails to wait. When they break in, Joe will call the police on my cellular phone. If the cops haven't arrived by the time the crooks come out of the building with the goods, I'll whistle. Then we'll hold them till the police arrive. That ought to give them a shock." He turned to Joe. "Did you check the phone?"

Joe nodded. "It's working fine," he said.

"I brought flashlights for everyone," Frank said.

"Just one thing," Bess said. "I don't want to go on one of those trails all by myself. It's going to be dark soon."

"Okay," Joe said. "You can come with me, Bess. There seem to be four trails, which leaves one of you for each of the remaining three. No way those guys can get in or out of here without one of us getting a good look at them."

"Unless we've got the wrong target," Frank reminded him. "It's not a sure thing, Joe, remember?"

"When we get in position, let's all flash our lights, okay?" Nancy suggested.

They all agreed and soon parted to find their trails. Nancy's led through dense woods filled with giant ferns. Rounding a bend, she froze in midstep.

Standing in front of her was a young man with wild dark eyes. In his left hand he held a bunch of giant yellow flowers.

In his right, high above his head, was a machete!

Chapter

Seven

HER HEART POUNDING, Nancy stared up at the machete blade, gleaming even in the fading light. It was poised, ready to slice her in half. Nancy watched in horror as the figure advanced slowly on her, raising the blade higher with each step. "Don't scream," he ordered, "or your neck will feel my blade!"

From his deeply tanned skin and dark eyes, Nancy guessed that he must be a native Hawaiian. His glossy black hair hung straight to his shoulders, and around his forehead was a rolled purple bandanna. "Who are you?" Nancy whispered.

"I am the spirit of old Hawaii," the young man

said mysteriously. "I am the will of my people!" Staring at her intently, he was still and calm.

"What do you want?" Nancy asked.

"I want the plunder to stop," he hissed.

"So do I," Nancy told him quietly.

"You? But you're one of them. Or why else are you here?" He continued to focus on her without seeming to blink.

"My name is Nancy," she said softly. "Nancy Drew. I'm here to help stop the art thefts on this island. I'm here because I want to see all royal treasures returned to the people of Hawaii."

The young man was torn. Obviously, he didn't want to believe a word she was saying, but just as obviously, he did. "Don't lie to me. My people have been lied to long enough."

Nancy now noticed that the blade of the machete was slowly being lowered. "I'm not lying," she told him. "I want to help. I can prove—"

Nancy was cut short by the man's harsh words. "Drop the flashlight to the ground," he ordered.

Nancy forced herself to remain calm, and did as he asked. He picked up the light and beamed it at her for what seemed forever. "You're an honest *wahine,*" he finally said.

"*Wa-hee-nee?*" she repeated, confused by the strange word.

"*Wahine* is Hawaiian for 'woman,'" he explained. "I see the spirit in your eyes now. It is true and clear. You are not one of them."

"And who are you?" Nancy asked gently.

"I am Luke Kilauea," he answered calmly.

"Kilauea? That's the name of the volcano on the Big Island. It isn't your real name. Is it?"

Luke nodded slowly. "Oh, yes. For generations. I am pure Hawaiian, full-blooded, like my parents and cousins. There aren't many of us left. We live on the island of Niihau."

"Niihau?" Nancy vaguely recalled the name, but she couldn't place it. "It's not one of the main Hawaiian Islands, I know that from my guidebook."

Luke's eyes flashed with contempt. "You will not find Niihau in guidebooks. This island is the forbidden island."

"What do you mean, 'forbidden'?"

"Niihau is privately owned, and the family who owns it has allowed us native Hawaiians to make it ours, and ours alone. We work on the family's plantation there and live our lives apart from the rest of the world. It's the last place where we can be truly Hawaiian, living with the earth, not on it."

His machete was resting harmlessly at his side, Nancy noticed, and any fear she'd had of him was gone. Luke had a rock solid quality that Nancy had seldom encountered before.

"I'm supposed to go to the end of this trail," she told him. "Come with me. I'll explain as we go." He followed her, and she confided the plan to him.

Luke nodded approvingly. "How many of you are there?" he asked.

"Five," Nancy said.

"It's a good plan," Luke said.

They had reached the trail's end. "May I have my flashlight back, please?" Nancy asked.

"Sure," Luke said, handing it to her.

Nancy flashed her light and three lights blinked back out of the darkness. The moon was just rising, casting a glow on the tiled roof of the mausoleum. Nancy had a perfect view of the tomb and the surrounding area.

"Everyone's in place and ready. Now we wait," Nancy said, dropping to the ground next to a giant fiddlehead fern. "What are those yellow flowers? Why are you carrying them?" They looked like the flowers she and George had seen earlier, at the scene of the murder.

"They are the flowers of the mao plant," he told her. "A native plant. But like so many native Hawaiian things, they are being destroyed by foreign invaders."

Nancy couldn't help thinking of Rachel Maxon, when she talked about the big corporations and the changes they brought. "It's not just plants that are being destroyed," she said sympathetically.

Luke settled on the ground next to her. "My islands are so beautiful, Nancy," he said, scooting closer to her. "But they are becoming more and more false. Soon the spirits of our ancestors who walk at night will not recognize their homeland! And now our treasure is being plundered, too. These thieves steal the wealth of all the people."

Nancy thought of Ana Saleo speaking about Rami Tanga and the way he had exploited the Torquesan Islands. "We're going to stop the thieves, Luke," she said quietly. "We're going to do everything in our power to find your treasures and return them to you."

"My people have mystic weapons—weapons the exploiter cannot see."

Though she didn't understand him, his heart-felt commitment inspired Nancy. The two sat in silence for a time. Then Luke handed Nancy a flower. "To some this is a simple plant and no more, but the wise man sees the power in it."

"Tell me," Nancy asked, "why are you carrying them?"

"Because here in the Nuuanu Valley is one of the few places left where the mao grows. I carefully harvest them, taking only as many as my father needs, so he can study them to try to save them."

"Your father lives on Niihau, too?" Nancy asked.

"Yes, he is a big man there."

"Big man." Joe had overheard Harry Leong say those same words. "What do you mean by that exactly?" Nancy asked.

"Kame Kilauea, my father, is a medicine man and shaman. People around the world know him as a man of great power and intelligence. Scientists seek his wisdom about healing plants and trees."

"And he's trying to save the mao," Nancy said, understanding.

Just then Nancy heard the sound of tires turning on the dirt road below. "Someone's here," Nancy whispered, alert and ready. She saw a long black car riding slowly down the main drive. In the moonlight and from a distance it appeared to be an old Lincoln Continental with the headlights doused. "That must be them!" Nancy whispered. Luke's hand went to the hilt of his machete.

Nancy watched the car pull up. The doors opened, and three masked figures emerged, silhouetted by the interior lights.

Nancy watched as the three people crept stealthily toward the entrance. Her heart pounding, she told herself to remain calm. Joe would be calling the police any second now.

"Aaaiiiiyyyyaaa!" Nancy froze in shock as Luke jumped up beside her and unleashed a bloodcurdling yell. Before she could stop him, he had bolted from their hiding place, pushed through the few trees around them, and was racing across the lawn in the moonlight. "Stop!" he shrieked, heading straight for the thieves. "Stop! Stop!"

"Luke, no!" Nancy yelled, but it was too late. Luke Kilauea was ruining everything!

Chapter

Eight

As Luke's scream pierced the quiet night, other cries rose to meet it. The masked thieves shouted as they scrambled back toward their car. Nancy's friends called out to one another, the beams from their flashlights bobbing wildly as they tore across the lawn. Nancy could tell in an instant that they'd never get to the thieves or Luke in time.

His machete raised high, Luke flew toward the three intruders. Two made it into the car, the third almost in.

"They're getting away!" Joe's voice rang out as the car's engine roared to life. It screeched into reverse. Flashlights were dropped as everyone ran to dodge the careening vehicle.

The third thief leapt for the car as the driver changed to a forward gear and managed to pull open the back door. As he was jumping in, Luke launched himself and grabbed a leg. "Yeow!" roared the masked figure. The voice sounded like a man's to Nancy.

The car bucked into gear. The third thief clutched the door with Luke dangling from his leg. Finally Luke couldn't hold on any longer. The car dragged the still-screaming thief twenty yards more before it stopped so he could throw himself in. The car then roared off into the night.

They all got up and dusted themselves off. After retrieving their flashlights, they met near the mausoleum.

Joe, who was holding Luke's machete, shone his flashlight into Luke's face. "Who are you?" he demanded. "And why did you ruin our stakeout like that?"

"Joe!" Nancy cried. "He's a friend!"

Confused, Joe stopped.

"I'm sorry," Luke said softly. "I thought I could capture them."

"Even if you had caught up to them, that wouldn't have helped. They hadn't committed the crime yet. What were you going to do with them?"

"I—I don't know," Luke said. "I guess I should have thought first."

"I guess you should have," Joe echoed bitterly. "By the way, who are you?"

"I told you, Joe," Nancy said, "he's a friend. I met him on the trail. His name is Luke Kilauea."

"And what's he doing there?" Joe demanded.

"I was here for the same reason you are," Luke said passionately. He told them what he'd told Nancy. Nancy could tell that Joe didn't believe a word Luke said.

Bess came forward, studying Luke in the light from all the flashlights. "He looks innocent to me!"

"Everybody looks innocent to you, Bess," Joe said.

"Well, he isn't wearing black clothes and a mask like those other three were," George pointed out. "And he did try to stop them."

"He could have been their lookout," Joe said hotly. "If he wasn't, he should have been. He did a great job of warning them. We didn't even get a chance to phone for help."

"Listen, I know you're upset," Nancy said to Frank and Joe, "but I think Luke was trying to help. And he may be able to help us solve that murder at the hotel. He knows about the flowers that were under the body. Luke is a native Hawaiian. His father is Kame Kilauea, a shaman who works with plants."

"Come to Niihau and see for yourself. I invite you all," Luke said, clearly trying to soothe the angry feelings he'd provoked. "Please come as my guests."

"Great," Joe muttered angrily. "Just great."

"We'd better go home," George suggested. "Do you have a car, Luke?"

"My motorbike is hidden in the bushes," he replied. "I'm staying with some relatives on Oahu in a little town called Maili. It's north of Honolulu."

After Nancy got a number where she could reach him, she and the others headed back to their hotels.

"Do you think they'll try to hit the mausoleum again? Or will they island-hop like they were planning?" Frank asked out loud.

"Beats me," Joe said. "If they're island-hopping, how do we find out where?" He sounded really down.

Nancy and the girls remained silent. They knew how badly Frank and Joe must have felt. They'd lost an important chance—maybe their last—to crack the case wide open.

"You know, I'm not even sure those people were Heather, Harry, and Willy," Joe said. "It was so dark, and they had those stupid masks on." He banged a fist against the dashboard of the car. "Why did that guy have to yell!"

"I don't know what to say," Frank muttered. "Whether Luke was in on it or not, it comes down to the same thing—we blew it bad."

Without much conversation, the Hardys drove back to the Grand Hawaiian.

"See you tomorrow," Frank said as he and Joe drove off.

66

"Can I finally get some dinner?" Bess asked as they stepped into the pink marble lobby.

"Definitely," George agreed. "I'm hungry myself. Let's not take the time to change."

"I have to check in with my dad," Nancy told them, "so I'll meet you in a couple of minutes. But go ahead and order me some Thai noodles, okay? And, Bess, if my dish comes before I get there, hands off!"

"Are you suggesting that I would steal your food?" Bess retorted in mock insult. Her tendency to take a generous "taste" of her friends' dinners was legendary.

"Watch her, George," Nancy ordered as she hurried for the elevators. When she arrived at her father's room, she found him sitting with Rachel Maxon. A bunch of papers was spread out on the coffee table in front of them.

"Hi," Nancy said. "How's your stomach, Rachel? You look a lot better."

"Oh, I am," Rachel said with a smile. "Your father has a very restorative effect on me, I guess." She and Carson gave each other a warm look.

"Nan, what's this I hear about your finding a dead body? I'm worried about you." Her father's face was concerned.

"I'm fine, Dad," Nancy assured him. Then she explained all that had happened.

"I see. And what about tonight? Where were you?" he asked, giving her a penetrating look.

"I was—out with the Hardys. Bess and George were there, too. We went for a drive." Well, that was true, at least as far as it went. Later, when they were alone, she'd tell him where she'd been and why.

"We even met a native Hawaiian who invited us to visit Niihau," she said, changing the subject.

"Niihau?" Carson asked.

"It's a small, private island, Carson, west of Kauai," Rachel told him. "I have a very distant relative who manages the macadamia nut plantation there. Who invited you, Nancy?"

"Luke Kilauea," Nancy said. As she spoke, she watched Rachel's face closely. "Do you know him?" she asked.

"I know his father, Kame Kilauea," Rachel said. "Anyone who's lived here all her life knows Big Man Kame. He loves this land, and he's worked tirelessly to preserve our heritage."

"Hey," Carson interrupted with a smile. "We were going to take a walk, remember?"

Rachel nodded and said, "Give me a few minutes to get a sweater. I'll meet you in the lobby."

After Rachel had left, Nancy said, "She's very good-looking, Dad."

"She's happy tonight because we managed to work out a new payment schedule for her taxes," Carson said.

"She seems pretty happy to be with you," Nancy pointed out.

"She's very sweet, Nancy," her father said. "But I don't really know her very well."

"I just want you to know that whatever makes you happy is fine with me. 'Cause you're the best," Nancy said.

"Well, it runs in the family," Carson said with a soft smile, squeezing her hand and releasing it.

"Gosh, I almost forgot! Bess and George are waiting for me to eat."

"You mean you haven't eaten yet?" Carson asked, straightening some of the papers in front of him.

"We got sidetracked," Nancy admitted. She hoped her father wouldn't ask any more, and fortunately, he didn't. "I'll ride down with you," he volunteered.

The elevator stopped on the third floor, and Ana Saleo stepped inside. "Ms. Saleo, I'm Nancy Drew," Nancy said excitedly, shaking the woman's slender hand. "Your speech last night was so inspiring. I promised myself to read up on Rami Tanga—everything I can get my hands on."

"I'm Carson Drew," Nancy's father broke in. "My daughter's a detective."

"Really!" Ana Saleo seemed genuinely impressed. "And so young. My, my. Well, I'm sorry to say we need an entire army of detectives to figure out how Tanga gets money out of his European bank accounts. One source in Europe tells me our money is there and that Tanga has been drawing on it. He does it all without leaving here—of that we're sure, too. I am shocked that your government continues to support him!"

"I sent a fax to my senator this afternoon," Carson said.

Ms. Saleo turned to him gratefully. "If more of you would do that, it would help. I'm sure of it."

"Quite a woman," Carson remarked after they parted at the lobby.

"She sure is," Nancy agreed. "And I'd hate it if she went back to the Torquesas empty-handed."

"Now don't get involved in that case, too," he said, warning her.

"Okay, I won't," Nancy said, with her fingers crossed behind her back. Nancy said good night to her father and turned to enter the café.

"Bess Marvin! Put that fork down this instant!" Nancy said, sweeping toward the table where Bess and George sat waiting for their dinner. The delicate scent of lemon grass drifting up from the pile of thin rice noodles made Nancy's mouth water.

"I was only going to take a taste," Bess protested. But Nancy knew otherwise.

"Just in the nick of time," George said as her dinner and Bess's were put on the table. For a few minutes all talking stopped as the three hungry girls ate their fill.

"What a day," George said eventually. "I'm exhausted and I want to get to bed early."

"Me, too," Bess agreed. "The surfing contest starts at eight on Makaha Beach."

As for Nancy, she planned on calling Luke first

thing in the morning. She'd already decided to accept his invitation to visit Niihau—tomorrow if possible. She hoped to learn more about Big Man Kame.

As soon as they had finished eating, the three friends headed upstairs to their beds.

"Night, everyone," George said sleepily as she slithered under the thin cotton blanket.

"Good night," Bess answered with a yawn, turning off the light by her bed.

Soon George and Bess were breathing steadily. Too full of questions, Nancy adjusted her pillow and thought. Her mind flitted from the evening's adventure to the dead man in the parking garage to her father and Rachel Maxon sitting so cozily on the couch together to Ana Saleo shaking her hand, saying her country needed people like Nancy. Then there was Luke, sitting in the lush greenery, telling her about old Hawaii, and his mystic secrets. . . .

What a day. Her mind a jumble, Nancy felt her body get heavier and sink into the clean sheets. She could feel the dreams coming on fast. . . .

Then she heard it—a sound that didn't belong in her dreams. The sound of a doorknob clicking as it was turned. Then the door slowly creaked open.

The door into their living room!

Holding her breath, Nancy propped herself up to check on Bess and George, who were fast asleep.

Who was out there?

Chapter

Nine

HER HEART POUNDING WILDLY, Nancy listened to someone move through the suite's sitting room. One of the feet sounded as if it was dragging. Did the person have a limp? Closer and closer the person moved across the carpeting.

Swallowing hard, Nancy made one desperate play. "Hello, security?" she said softly, but loud enough for the person to hear. "There's an intruder in Suite four-twenty-five. You'll be right up? Oh, thank you!" The phone was across the bedroom next to Bess, and Nancy just hoped the intruder wouldn't call her bluff.

A few seconds later the front door squeaked open again, and the intruder retreated. Her plan had worked!

Instantly Nancy was out of bed, running from the bedroom to the outer room of the suite. She threw the door open and peered out. A man with a limp was rushing down the hall toward the elevator. Before Nancy could tell anything else about him, the elevator doors swallowed him up.

Examining the lock on her door, she detected no damage. Could the visitor work at the hotel? This was the second time someone had gotten into one of their rooms and the electronic card security system had been broken.

While Bess and George continued to sleep peacefully, Nancy checked the outer room. The coat closet door was open, and George's willow beach bag had been overturned. Once again, Nancy surmised, the intruder had come for something—but what?

Had he found it? If he hadn't, would he be back again? That thought shot through Nancy like an electric current. Switching off the light, she returned to the darkened bedroom and slipped back into bed. There was no sense alarming Bess and George. The intruder would not be back that night, Nancy was sure.

When the first light came through the window, Nancy dialed Rachel's suite. "Sorry to call so early, but I need to see you right away," she said quietly because her friends were still asleep.

"Of course, Nancy," Rachel replied. "Come to my suite. It's number one-oh-five, next to my office."

Nancy hurried downstairs, where Rachel greeted her in a blue silk robe pulled tight at the waist. "Twice in two days," she gasped after Nancy told her about the intruder. "I'd better get my security chief in here." Picking up the phone she tapped a couple of digits. "Send Johnny Leong to one-oh-five right away."

Leong. That name was familiar. Harry Leong was one of the Hardys' prime suspects in the thefts, Nancy recalled. "How common a name is Leong here in Hawaii?" Nancy asked.

"Fairly common," Rachel answered. "Why? Do you know someone by that name?" Before Nancy could answer, a knock interrupted them. "Johnny, come in," Rachel said, pulling the door open.

Nancy watched as a thin, nervous-looking man made his way inside—limping!

"There's been another break-in," Rachel explained, giving him the details. "Naturally, I'm very upset about it, extremely upset. In both cases, the card code system failed completely. You promised me that system was the very best!"

The security chief shot her a hard look. "Are you saying I had something to do with the break-ins?" he challenged.

"Look, Johnny, all I know is that hotel security is your responsibility," Rachel replied wearily. "As of today, I'm suspending you until I find out what's going on around here. Sorry, but I have to."

Johnny Leong gave her a faintly amused look then muttered, "Whatever you feel is best."

"I think it would be best for you to clear your desk today and not come back until further notice."

"Fine," Johnny Leong said. He cast a sidelong glance at Nancy and left the room.

"This is the one part of being an executive that I don't really like," Rachel said. "But I won't feel comfortable with him around, not knowing what's happening. Nancy, I promise to look into this matter."

"Are you okay?" Nancy asked.

"I'll be fine," Rachel said, rubbing her midsection.

"Is he from around here?" Nancy asked.

"His father was from the Torquesas and his mother was Hawaiian," Rachel said. "He's been my security chief for about six months now."

"I hope you have better luck with your next security chief," Nancy said, getting up to leave.

After Nancy said goodbye, she walked to the lobby and called Luke, to make arrangements to visit Niihau. He said he couldn't join them but insisted they go anyway. After Nancy hung up, she headed to the hotel café. George and Bess were up and helping themselves to the exotic fruits and oversize muffins that made up the breakfast buffet. "Hi, guys," Nancy said, joining them. "How'd you sleep?"

"Great." Bess smiled. "How about you?"

"Do you really want to know?" Nancy began. With a wry grin, she told them what they'd missed.

"You're kidding!" George said, astonished to learn about the intruder. "We slept through all that?"

"We said we were exhausted," Bess put in. "I guess we were right."

"I've just lost my appetite," George said, pushing her half-eaten breakfast away. "I'll be glad to get off this island today. Hopefully it will be more peaceful on Niihau."

"Hey, what about me?" Bess said. "I'm staying here, remember?"

"Willy will take care of you, Bess," George teased.

"Yeah," Nancy added with a twinkle in her eye. "Try to get a full confession out of him about the art thefts while you're at it."

Bess rolled her eyes and shook her head. "I'm telling you, Willy's not involved in these thefts. The only thing he's interested in is surfing!"

"Speaking of Willy, there he is," George murmured, pointing to the veranda that led to the café. "I think he's looking for you, Bess."

Bess swung around, and a giant smile came over her face. "Willy!" She waved. "Over here."

As the surfer took steps toward them, Nancy let out a gasp. Willy was limping!

"What happened to your foot?" Bess asked as he reached their table.

"Not much," he said. "I twisted my ankle yesterday—surfing."

"I don't remember you limping yesterday," Nancy pressed.

"It stiffened up last night," Willy said flatly. Then he turned to Bess and cocked his head. "Bess, can we talk in private?"

"Sure," Bess said. "Is something wrong?"

She stood up and joined him, and they walked out of earshot. A few minutes later Bess was heading back to the table, and Willy was leaving the restaurant. His hands were deep in the pockets of his baggy shorts.

"What nerve!" Bess said hotly. "You know, I hate to say it, but Joe Hardy was right. Willy Brannigan is a jerk!"

"What happened, Bess?" Nancy asked.

"He said he doesn't want me to come to the contest today," Bess said, tears welling up in her eyes. "He said it makes him nervous when I'm there."

"Nervous?" George repeated, in disbelief. "That's weird."

"I don't believe it," Bess said. "After all, I was there yesterday and he won, right? Maybe he has another girl coming today."

"Poor Bess," George said sympathetically. "I know you really liked him, too."

"Wait a minute," Bess shot back defensively. "I didn't like him *that* much."

Nancy had to smile at her friend's resilience.

No guy could ever get Bess down for long. "Want to come with us to Niihau, Bess? I called Luke, and we're visiting his dad today."

"Of course, I'm coming," Bess said, reaching for her papaya drink. "I'd much rather go to a new island than hang out at some dumb surfing contest. Surfing is boring."

"Surfing is boring? What's this I hear?" came Frank Hardy's voice as he and Joe approached the table. "Is it true, Joe? Surfing is boring?"

"Maybe for the spectators," Joe said with a smile as he pulled up a chair from an empty table and sat down. "How's everyone this morning?"

"You seem pretty cheerful, Joe," Nancy observed. "You were kind of down last night."

"Hey, it's a brand-new day," Joe said. "Things can only get better. How about you guys?"

There was a second of silence, and then Nancy volunteered, "Our room was broken into by a man with a limp."

Joe let out a low whistle while Nancy filled the Hardys in. When he heard the part about Johnny Leong, Frank folded his arms. "Leong, huh? I wonder if there's a connection to Harry. You say he limped?"

"Yes, but wait until you hear this," George put in. "Willy Brannigan was also limping today."

"Maybe it was Willy's leg Luke grabbed last night," Bess suggested.

"Wait a minute, Bess," Joe said, "you're mixing up two cases. The break-ins at your suite are probably connected to the murder, remember? Not the thefts."

Nancy drummed her fingers on the tabletop. "Unless they're connected in a way we don't understand yet," she said. That thought stopped their conversation cold.

Frank leaned in close to speak. "Well, one thing's for sure—we'd better stay alert today. If the thieves are Heather, Harry, and Willy, or anyone actually, they know we're after them. And obviously, someone is after the three of you because they think you have something that's important to them."

"What are you girls doing today?" Joe asked.

"We're going to Niihau to meet with Luke's father," Nancy told him.

"Is Luke going to be there?" George asked.

"No," Nancy replied. "He has to stay on Oahu. I hope he isn't doing any snooping on his own. He's not very good at it. Anyway, he told me how to get to Niihau. Speaking of which, we'd better get going. We've got a plane to catch."

After they said their goodbyes, Nancy and her friends hurried to their Jeep in the underground parking lot. A barrier of bright yellow plastic tape surrounded the area where the dead man had been found. On the ground, an outline of smudged white chalk indicated where the corpse had fallen.

"Ugh, that gives me the creeps," Bess said.

Driving out of the lot into the bright Hawaiian

sun had a cheering effect on them all. "Look at that sky," George said dreamily. "It's a beautiful day."

"Seems like every day is beautiful in Hawaii," Nancy agreed. At the airport they purchased tickets for their short flight.

At the departure gate a uniformed man came and introduced himself with a jaunty smile. "Hi there, girls. I'm Captain Wingate. You're off to Niihau, eh? Great place! What made you decide to go there?"

"We want to find out about these weird yellow—" Bess began, but Nancy deftly cut her off.

"Sunsets. Our friends told us they're better on Niihau than anywhere else in Hawaii."

Wingate seemed a little confused by Nancy's strange response, but he smiled broadly nevertheless. "Well, not many tourists get to Niihau— unless they have a particular reason for going." The captain seemed to be waiting for them to volunteer more. When they didn't, he said, "We'll be flying in a six-seater today. You'll be my only passengers. Lucky for me."

Again the captain waited, and again the girls were quiet. Finally he walked away. "See you on board," he called back over his shoulder. "Fifteen minutes, okay?"

"I don't trust that guy," George said.

"Me, neither," Bess added.

"That makes three of us," Nancy agreed. "Excuse me, you two," she told her friends, following a hunch and taking off after the pilot.

Which way had he gone? Glancing toward the pay phones, Nancy didn't see the pilot. She walked down the hallway a little farther, then turned down a quiet side corridor, with several unmarked doors on either side.

Hearing the pilot's voice behind one of them, she put her ear to the door. She couldn't make out all the words, but she could tell there was another man in the room. "I'm trying!" the captain was saying. Nancy heard chairs being scraped back as the pilot said, "See you this afternoon." Backing away from the door, Nancy crossed the hall to the ladies' room and opened it. She stayed in the doorway and peered out around the frame.

When the captain emerged from the room with another man, Nancy blinked hard. Wingate's companion was someone she recognized. In fact, she had met him for the first time that very morning.

Johnny Leong!

Nancy swallowed hard, suddenly worried about herself and her friends. Was there going to be trouble on their flight or their visit to Niihau?

Chapter

Ten

Nancy went back to the gate, where Bess and George were waiting. Wingate soon joined them and led them across the asphalt to the small plane they'd be traveling in.

"It's so tiny," Bess said nervously. "Like a car with wings."

"Just climb in, Bess," George said.

Soon Honolulu lay below them with the deep blue Pacific lapping at its shore.

"I love it!" George shouted over the roar of the small engine. "You can see everything from up here!"

Nancy was only half-aware of the view. She was a lot more concerned about why Leong had been meeting with the pilot and if it had anything to do with the case.

"Look up ahead on your left—we'll be coming past Chinaman's Hat," the captain shouted. "It's a rock formation in the water. See it?"

Nancy peered out and saw the huge formation set like an onyx rock in the bright sea.

They passed over Oahu and crossed more water to another island. "That must be Kauai," Nancy volunteered. "They call it the Green Island."

"I can see why," shouted Bess, staring at the verdant mountaintops.

"It rains there a lot," the captain explained loudly. "In fact, the northwest coast is one of the wettest spots on earth."

Close to the coast of Kauai, another smaller island came into view. "Is that Niihau?" George yelled.

"Yes, indeed," he returned. "That's Niihau, the forgotten Hawaiian Island, the one most tourists don't even know about."

"Niihau, the sacred island," Nancy murmured quietly, thinking of Luke and his faith in the ways of his people.

Only George heard her. Wingate was busy navigating, and Bess's nose was pressed against the window on the other side of the craft. "I see a field of pink!" she cried happily. "What is it?"

"That's an orchid farm," the pilot told her. "Here on Niihau, the people don't want any polluting industries. So they grow nuts, taro plant, and flowers. Take a deep breath, because I'm going to bring this baby down."

After landing at the small airstrip, Wingate told them to be back at five for the return trip. "And please don't be late," the pilot said. "Just before we took off, a man hired me for a private flight at seven."

Nancy realized that Leong must have hired him. But it seemed too coincidental that he'd shown up at the exact same time as Nancy and her friends.

The girls left the small airport building and stepped out into the balmy air. "Kame is going to meet us," Nancy told her friends.

But instead, a girl of about six ran up to them. In her hands were three glorious red garlands of hibiscus flowers. She handed one to each of them. "Thank you," Nancy told her warmly.

"Grandfather said, walk with me," she said confidently, taking Nancy by the hand. "My name is Kali."

"Your grandfather is Kame Kilauea?" Nancy asked, smiling down at Kali.

"Yes." The girl nodded and led them away from the airport down a narrow unpaved road. Above them, puffy white clouds dotted the sky.

"The air is so great here," George said, breathing deeply.

Bess reached down and picked up a fallen hibiscus blossom, which she put behind her ear. "Where does your grandfather live? Is it far?"

The little girl didn't answer. She kept walking, holding Nancy's hand tightly. As they neared a small cement building with the words General Supplies stenciled on it, a man of about fifty emerged from inside, carrying a grocery bag. His large frame carried a considerable amount of fat, and he wore a garland of small shells around his neck.

"Aloha, and welcome to our island," he said, stepping forward to greet Nancy and her friends. "I am Kame Kilauea, and I am very grateful for your help in trying to save our Hawaiian treasures. I offer my sincere thanks. Come!"

He ushered them to his car, an old sedan dating from the 1970's. The group piled in, and within five minutes they pulled up in front of a clapboard house surrounded by palm trees and thick bougainvillea bushes. Kali ran off to play behind the house. Craning her neck, Nancy noticed an immense greenhouse there.

"Later I will show you my laboratory," he said. "But first you must meet my wife. She's waiting in the garden. Come."

He led the girls around the far side of the house. There, Nancy's eyes were caught by a large pile of stones, about the size of a small tepee. "What's that?" she asked curiously. Some of the stones, she noticed, were carved with strange symbols.

"This, my child, is an altar. It was built by my people long ago. The rocks stand for the force of nature, which my people strive to obey."

"It's fascinating," George said. "May I touch it?"

"Yes," the old man answered with a laugh. "There is no distance between us and our gods. We may touch and feel them freely."

"Do people still worship at these altars?" Nancy asked.

"Very few," came Kame's sad answer. "Many have forgotten the old ways. Most altars have gone to ruin."

"These symbols are beautiful," George said. "What do they mean?"

Kame rubbed his fingers over a set of markings etched in one of the stones on the altar. "These are petroglyphs. Our ancestors carved their prayers into rock so they would be heard forever. Their meaning is of great importance. 'The land is sacred,'" he added in a near whisper. "You can see these markings throughout the islands, at altars and temples, on the faces of cliffs—at all the holy places where Pele is worshipped."

"I've heard of Pele. She's the goddess of fire, isn't she?" Bess asked.

"Pele," Kame told her, "rules from the inside of the earth. She rules the volcanoes. My people believe that she will free the people from false values and take revenge on those who harm the earth."

When he spoke, the man's dark eyes shone. His deep convictions and passion for nature made him appear young again.

He led them past the altar to the back of the

house. A petite woman with streaks of white in her jet black hair was kneeling beside a bed of flowering herbs. She wore a loose cotton dress, covered with painted designs.

"This is my Tika," Kame said with a smile.

"Aloha," she said, smiling warmly as they introduced themselves. Tika stood and nodded, pointing to a small table, the trowel still in her hand. "Come, we have mangoes from our tree and fresh poi."

"Poi?" Bess repeated. Nancy gave her a sharp look. "Sounds delicious," Bess added, getting the message.

"It's been the staff of life of our people for ages," Kame explained, laughing. "It's made from taro root. If you don't like it, please don't eat it. Many of our guests say it takes getting used to."

Nancy saw a small outdoor table that had been set up for them. Five cloth napkins were set inside five shallow wooden bowls. In the center of the table was an array of fruit and bread.

As a bird sang nearby, Kame and Tika asked the girls about their impressions of Hawaii. Luke's parents were relaxed and easy to be with. It was the perfect lunch in the perfect garden, Nancy thought, savoring more of the succulent fruit.

When they finished eating, Nancy turned to Big Man Kame. "What can you tell me about the mao plant?" she asked.

"I can do more than tell, I can show you this

plant." Turning to Tika, he grinned mischievously. "If my wife will generously clean the table now, I will do so tonight at supper."

Tika nodded playfully, and Kame led the girls into his greenhouse. The humid air inside was filled with the earthy, rich scent of flowers and loam. A long, low table was piled waist-high with leafy, dark green plants, many in brilliant golden flower.

"Mao, all mao," he said, indicating the plants with his arm. "My people believe the flower cools the fire of the body. We make a tea from it that tastes bitter but soothes the digestion. Science confirms our mystic knowledge. Many think the mao flower will soon offer an important defense against gastritis and other stomach ailments."

"I read a newspaper article about another plant with healing power," Bess said. "The article said twenty-five percent of all modern drugs come from plants."

Kame nodded. "Many, many plants have healing powers, child. The creator is wise, but man is sometimes foolish. He has built roads and houses on the land where the mao used to grow. There are very few left."

"You seem to have quite a lot of them here," Nancy noted. "What do you do with them?"

"I plant the seeds and send the blossoms to Switzerland," Kame told her, walking over to a small wooden desk on the far end of the greenhouse. "There, European scientists are learning to extract their power."

When Kame reached down to pick up a packing envelope to show Nancy, she caught her breath. The mailer was identical to the one George had found by the dead man!

"May I see that?" she asked, walking over to him and examining the large yellow address label. In deep purple ink it read, "From Kilauea Research Center, Niihau, Hawaii." The label also had a few petroglyph symbols, like the ones Kame had shown them on the altar.

"This mailer is addressed to a company called Futurehealth of Zurich, but the address is a post office box in Honolulu," Nancy noted, memorizing the box number—1119. "Why would a Swiss institute have a Honolulu address?"

Kame shrugged. "I suppose they ship from there."

"Haven't you ever met them?" Nancy asked.

"No, they contacted me by mail after my work was shown in the news," Kame answered. "I do not travel to Oahu. From what they said, it seems they are doing good work."

Leaving the greenhouse, the man turned to his guests. "Now I must ask you a favor. My grandchildren, Luke's nieces and nephews, have prepared an entertainment for you. Will you come hear them sing and watch them dance?"

"That would be fantastic," Bess said. Nancy nodded absentmindedly. How could one of Kame's mailers have gotten to the scene of the murder, she wondered. Could Kame be a "big man" in more than just medicine and healing plants?

Frank Hardy spread more turquoise goo over his nose. Thank goodness for sunblock, he thought. Without it he'd resemble a cooked lobster. He'd been out in the hot sun for over six hours supposedly watching the surfing contest. His attention, in fact, had been on Willy Brannigan, Heather Farwell, and Harry Leong.

Willy was sitting out the competition, his ankle wrapped in an orange neon bandage. All day he'd flirted with the girls, every so often calling out friendly insults to the other surfers, especially "Wipeout" Keenan.

Willy's cracks were getting to Joe, Frank noticed. His brother kept signing on for more and more surf time, even though he wasn't performing very well. "Take it easy out there," Frank had warned him earlier. "We need you in one piece."

Joe's whole intent seemed to be to show Willy he could surf with the best. Just then he was out there fighting another wave.

"Hi," came a sweet voice next to Frank's ear. He turned and saw Heather Farwell's sharp blue eyes smiling at him. "Can I talk to you?"

All day Heather had been throwing Frank smiles and coy looks, but he had ignored them. "Go ahead," he said with a shrug.

Heather slid onto the sand next to Frank and let out a sigh. "I'm really, really sorry about what happened when we were at Surf Riders."

"That's nice of you," Frank said flatly.

"Why don't you believe me?" she asked, pouting.

Maybe it was instinct that made Frank turn around, or maybe he figured she was wasting his time on purpose. Sure enough, there were Willy and Harry across the road, heading for the parking lot. Heather was attempting to distract him.

"I want to explain about the other day," she said.

Well, thought Frank. That should be interesting. Except that he had to get out of there right then and go after the other two.

"How about a little later," Frank said, getting to his feet. "Right now I've got to pick up a pizza." Heather showed surprise at that one. "See you later," he added, with a little wave. "Make sure no one walks off with my towel. Okay?"

Before she could object, Frank was gone. Within ten minutes he was on the highway, two cars behind Harry. It was an easy tail job. The coast road had no turnoffs for at least seven miles, and there was just enough traffic to cover him.

"Whoa," Frank murmured, when Harry turned off at the Honolulu airport sign. What was this all about? What if Harry and Willy were going to meet Nancy, Bess, and George? If they were, it wasn't likely to be a friendly reception.

Frank watched as Willy and Harry approached a Jeep and stopped.

Frank parked and slid out. After closing his door as quietly as he could, he edged closer for a better look.

Willy stood and scanned the parking lot, making sure nobody was watching. Then he nodded to Harry, who reached into his belt and pulled out a long switchblade. With swift, short strokes, the bouncer started to slash the upholstery of the Jeep.

Frank noticed a sticker of a car rental company above the back bumper. Seeing a flamingo pink beach towel draped over the backseat, next to a straw hat with a pink band, Frank felt a sick feeling grow in his stomach. That was Bess's hat. And the Jeep they were vandalizing was Nancy Drew's!

Chapter

Eleven

HIDDEN BEHIND a maroon Dodge Caravan, Frank watched in amazement as Willy joined Harry in slashing up the seats. He stopped periodically and ran his hand under the upholstery, feeling for something. Harry stopped and knelt down to look at the underside of the vehicle.

Apparently, neither of them found what he wanted. Willy got out of the Jeep and kicked a tire. Harry pulled himself out from underneath, cursing. Then the two headed for the terminal, several hundred yards away. Harry strode forcefully with Willy right behind him, only slightly slowed by his limp.

Frank followed immediately. He had just been jolted into a new and startling realization. The murder and art thefts were connected! Not only that, Harry and Willy were involved in both. How did it all work? Where was the real connection?

Worst of all, Frank thought, if Willy and Harry had just slashed up a Jeep, what were they about to do to the girls?

Frank bolted for the terminal. He had to know where they were going. Inside, he thought he saw Harry moving toward the gates. Frank took off after him but had trouble getting through the crowd. A large tour group was making its way toward Frank.

Frank plowed on, then stopped when he caught a flash of reddish blond hair. "Nancy!" he called, as she emerged from the rest room with George and Bess.

"Frank, what are you doing here?" The girls looked happy and refreshed from their day's outing.

"Boy, am I glad to see that you guys are okay." Frank breathed a sigh of relief. "No problems on Niihau?"

Nancy shook her head. "No, everything went fine," she said. "Although at first I thought the pilot may have been keeping an eye on us for Johnny Leong. Turns out Leong hired him for a private trip."

"Speaking of Leongs, Harry and Willy are here in the airport. They were just outside, trashing your Jeep, in fact."

"What do you mean trashing it?" George asked.

"They ripped the interior to shreds," Frank told them. "Then they went that-a-way." He pointed down the corridor toward the gates. "Looking for you, I guess." The crowd was pretty much gone by now.

"Those creeps!" Bess said. "Did they rip up my hat, too?"

Before Frank could answer, Nancy gave him a small push. "Quick. Here they come!" she cried softly. "Let's disappear."

The girls ducked back into the ladies' room, and Frank moved across the hall to the men's. Keeping the door open a crack, Frank spied Willy and Harry walking back down the corridor. They seemed to be arguing.

Frank waited until the two were safely past. Then he went over to the ladies' room door. "All clear," he said. As the girls emerged, he added, "I guess they'll head on out of here now. They must figure they missed you."

Bess shivered despite the heat. "What do we do now?" she asked.

"For starters, we'd better call the rental car company and tell them what happened," Nancy suggested.

George and Bess went off to phone, and Frank turned to Nancy. "I guess our two cases really are related."

"This business with the Jeep makes it pretty

clear," Nancy said. "Frank, I may have a lead. There's a post office box that Kame Kilauea's been sending mao flowers to. He says they go to a Swiss research company, but it sounds fishy to me."

"Anything else?" Frank asked.

"Remember that first day we talked, you told me Joe overheard Harry talking about 'the big man'?"

"What about it?"

"Who can the big man be? Big probably doesn't refer to size. So it must refer to the big boss of the ring."

What Nancy was saying made sense. Small-time thugs like Harry and Willy had to be working under someone if they were to succeed in robbing the state of its most priceless treasures.

"Good news," Bess said cheerfully, interrupting Frank's thoughts. "The guy at the rental agency's reporting the damage and said we should wait by the Jeep. They'll bring us a replacement."

"Okay, let's see how bad it is," Nancy said, steeling herself to see the damage.

"Wow," Bess said when they reached the Jeep. "I wonder why they didn't slash the tires and turn it over while they were at it."

"They probably didn't have time," Nancy said. "If they were planning to meet us at the gate, that is. Lucky thing we got in early."

Suddenly Frank remembered that Joe was still

at the beach. "Oh, no," he cried. "Joe must be wondering where I've gone."

Bess looked at her watch. "It's so late," she said. "Don't you think he got a lift home from somebody?"

"Or if he survived the competition?" George added. "You ought to check, Frank. Come on, I'll ride with you."

"I don't know," Frank said hesitantly. "I don't want to leave you girls alone."

"It's okay," Nancy said with a laugh. "Bess can defend us if anyone gives us any trouble. Right, Bess?"

Making a muscle, Bess clenched her teeth and raised her arm bravely.

"Seriously," Nancy said, "I don't think Harry or Willy will show up here again. They'll figure that we reported the damage to our Jeep, and they'll want to be far away."

"I guess so," Frank said. "Okay, George, let's go."

"See you guys later," George said, and walked off with Frank.

"My car's over here," Frank told her, leading her to the spot. "Want to ride with the top down?"

"Sure," George said. Soon they were driving down the highway with a warm breeze in their faces.

"The views are incredible," she said, staring out at the ocean. "Is Makaha a big beach?"

"You'll see it soon," he answered.

"It's great when there's no traffic, isn't it?" George said.

"I'll say," Frank agreed.

Rounding the next bend, he had to steer his car off the narrow highway. "What in the world?" he murmured.

There, parked across the road, was a big boat of a car, a Lincoln Continental with its hood up. The sprawling Lincoln completely blocked the highway.

"If it's overheated, why don't they push it off the road?" Frank asked, annoyed.

"Maybe it was in an accident?" George said, sounding as if she didn't think it had been.

"Shall we help?" Frank said, pushing his door open as George did, too.

"Frank!" George said, afraid. Frank turned and saw two masked men approaching from the opposite side of the road. Each of them carried a semiautomatic rifle in his burly arms.

"Hey! Wait a minute," Frank said, holding up his palms. The men responded by raising their weapons higher and setting their sights.

"No!" Frank shouted as George screamed.

The rifle went off with a soft *ping*. Frank watched, horrified, as George slowly crumpled to the ground.

"George!" he yelled, starting off around the front of the car to her. He had only a fraction of a second to wonder why there had been no loud bang. Then the *ping* sounded again, and the whole world went black.

Chapter

Twelve

Bᴇss ʟᴇᴀɴᴇᴅ ᴀɢᴀɪɴsᴛ the front of the Jeep and shook out her hair. Then she paced nervously around the vehicle. "I hope the guy from the rental agency gets here soon," she said.

"Bess," Nancy said gently, "why don't you go buy a newspaper and some magazines?" Clearly, Bess was scared about waiting and needed a diversion.

"Really?" Bess said, brightening for only a moment. "But I can't leave you here all alone."

Nancy grinned and shook her head. "Bess, I'll be fine. You go."

"But what if—"

"They won't come back," Nancy assured her.

"I think they made a pretty thorough search of this poor Jeep, don't you?"

"I guess you're right," Bess agreed. "But be careful, okay?"

Maybe the thieves had missed something, Nancy thought. But what? She tried to imagine what the murdered man might have done in his last minutes.

The man is running, she thought, running away from the guy with the gun. He sees he's cornered in the parking lot, so he ducks down beside our Jeep. If he has a gun, that's when he fires it.

"And then what?" Nancy asked herself out loud, staring at the Jeep. "He's crouched down, like this." She knelt beside the Jeep. "He's got this package with the flowers and a briefcase chained to his wrist. He undoes the handcuff to the briefcase, then opens it, takes whatever it is out. Now he has to hide it. . . ."

Playing out the fantasy, Nancy pulled out an imaginary package and, reaching under the Jeep, tried to stash it somewhere. She felt along the undercarriage, but there was nothing there. She lay on her back and pulled herself under the car to see if she had missed anything. That was when her eyes widened with surprise.

There *was* something stuffed under there, up in the chassis! Yanking it out, Nancy found herself holding a thick block of thousand-dollar bills! The bills were shrink-wrapped in clear plastic. There had to be a hundred of them—maybe more. "Wow!" Nancy said. She was holding over a million dollars!

Just then Nancy felt a hand on her leg and nearly jumped out of her skin. "Ow!" Nancy cried as she hit her head under the car. Quickly scrambling, she backed out from under the vehicle.

"Thank goodness you're okay!" Bess cried as Nancy slid out. "I saw your legs, and I thought something terrible had happened!"

Nancy massaged what would soon be a large bump on her head, raised herself up, and thrust out her hands to Bess.

Bess's jaw dropped as she stared at what was in Nancy's hands. Then she started squealing happily, jumping up and down. "Nancy, this is fantastic! We're rich!"

Nancy had to laugh, despite the seriousness of the situation. Bess had missed the meaning of the discovery. "Bess," Nancy reminded her, "*this* is what the criminals are after."

Bess's hand flew to her mouth. "Oh," she cried. "Of course." Suddenly Bess put a firm hand on Nancy's arm. "We have to get rid of this money right away, Nancy."

"We will, Bess. As soon as we can get to the police." Emptying the carry-all bag she'd taken with her to Niihau, Nancy just managed to stuff the money packet in and zip the bag shut.

A honking startled both Nancy and Bess. Spinning around, they saw a shiny red Jeep pull up.

"Nancy Drew?" the blond rental agent asked.

When Nancy nodded, the woman held out a set of keys for her. "Here's your new vehicle. I just need you to sign this sheet and give me the keys to the old one." She handed Nancy a clipboard with a printed form and a pen attached. "The insurance will cover the damages."

"That's a relief," Nancy said, signing the form.

A few minutes later Nancy and Bess took off, heading back to the Grand Hawaiian.

"As soon as we get back," Nancy said, veering onto the main road toward Honolulu, "we have to call Captain Morita and ask him to come get the money."

"Why not just bring it in to police headquarters?" Bess asked.

"Because I want to find out a few things from the captain before I hand over the money," Nancy explained. "And I'd rather talk on our turf than his."

Bess let out a heartfelt sigh. "So much for buying out the boutiques in the Grand Hawaiian. They have such cool stuff there, too. Did I tell you about the shell jewelry I saw? It was really neat—"

Nancy half-listened to Bess, her mind on the case. As long as they remained in Hawaii, she realized, she and her friends would be in danger. Whatever forces were responsible for the death of the man in the parking lot, the teens seemed to be players in a ruthless, high-stakes game of life and death.

Soon Nancy and Bess arrived back at their

hotel. "This time, I'm parking on the street," Nancy said.

Upstairs, Bess stashed the money under her mattress while Nancy phoned the police.

"Captain Morita will be here in twenty minutes," Nancy told Bess, hanging up. "I think I'll call my dad and let him know what's happening."

"Call room service and order some sandwiches, too," Bess suggested. "I'll have a grilled swiss."

Fortunately Carson was in his suite. "I'm here going over some papers with Rachel," he said. When he heard the news, he told Nancy he'd be right there.

"We'll all feel more comfortable when the police take the money away," Nancy said to her dad and Rachel Maxon when they arrived.

Captain Morita came soon after the sandwiches, which a hungry Bess and Nancy had gobbled up. After a quick nod to Rachel and Bess, and a brief introduction to Carson, the captain turned his attention to Nancy. "Okay, what's this 'new evidence'?"

"Before I show you," Nancy said, "I'd like to know what you've found out about the murder so far. There hasn't been anything in the papers."

The captain glanced uneasily at Rachel and Carson. "As a matter of fact, we're pursuing leads that demand we hold off on publicity."

"Such as?" Nancy pressed on.

The captain eyed Nancy closely, then let out an

annoyed sigh. "Such as, we know the identity of the dead man. His name was Felix Hoffman. He was a Swiss national who worked for a large firm in Zurich."

"Was the name of the firm Futurehealth by any chance?" Nancy asked, playing a hunch.

"Futurehealth? What's that?" the captain wanted to know.

"A research institute," Nancy explained.

"No, no," the captain said, impatiently. "Hoffman worked for a bank."

"Swiss banks are notorious for hiding illegally made money," Carson said to Bess. "It's known as laundering. Dirty money goes in, clean money comes out. And it's all done in total privacy."

"Anyway," the captain went on, "we know the victim had a briefcase because of the courier's bracelet on his wrist. He was probably murdered for whatever was in that case. But unfortunately, the thief got away with the contents."

"Not quite," Nancy said, interrupting. Stepping into the bedroom, she pulled out the money and carried it back to the stunned officer. "Here," she said. "Hoffman must have hidden this in our Jeep before he was shot. We found it about an hour ago."

"Someone else is actively hunting for it, though, Captain," Carson added. "The suites where the girls have stayed have been broken into twice."

Morita's eyes flashed to Rachel.

"I didn't report those incidents because I

thought we could handle them internally," Rachel explained, flustered. "The last thing this hotel needs right now is bad publicity."

"I understand," the captain said, his gaze returning to the money. "I bet this will trace back to the bank Hoffman worked for."

"Just one more thing, Captain," Nancy said as he turned to face her. "I have reason to believe that the murder is related to the recent rash of art thefts."

"Would you care to explain?" the captain said, confused.

"Well, for starters, how about this: our room was broken into by a man with a limp. Coincidentally, one of—" Nancy was interrupted by the phone. "Excuse me," she told the others, reaching for the receiver.

"Hello?" Nancy said.

"Nancy Drew?" The voice was raspy and distorted. Nancy couldn't make out whether it was male or female.

"Yes, this is Nancy Drew," she said, fear shooting through her.

"Are you alone?" said the voice, taking on a threatening tone.

Raising a hand for everyone in the room to be silent, Nancy answered quietly. "Yes. I'm alone. What do you want to tell me?"

"It's very simple," said the voice. "We have your friends—George Fayne and Frank Hardy. Listen closely or you'll never see them alive again."

Chapter

Thirteen

NANCY HEARD heavy breathing on the phone. Then she realized it was her own, coming fast and hard. "Yes?" she whispered, and then swallowed. "I'm listening. Go on."

She told herself to remain alert, to remember every word that might provide a clue. "You have something that belongs to us," said the rasping voice. "Am I right?"

Nancy bit her lip. This was no time to lie, not when Frank and George were in danger. "Er, yes, I have it," Nancy said, playing it straight.

"Well, we want it," the voice growled. "We'll call you tomorrow morning at eleven to tell you where and when to drop it off. You'll follow our instructions, then leave Hawaii within twelve hours—you *and* your other two companions. Once your plane is in the air, your friends will be released—unharmed."

"All right," Nancy said, her equilibrium returning. "But how do I know you're telling the truth? I want to speak to my friends."

Nancy heard a hand being placed over the mouthpiece, then she heard a man's voice say, "Bring her here." The sounds grew clear once again, and Nancy heard someone moan. Then George's voice came on, sounding foggy and only half-conscious. "What? Who? Nancy . . . ?"

"George!" Nancy shouted into the phone, forgetting herself. "Where are you, George?"

"Don't even try to find out," came the rasping voice over the receiver. "Understand this, Miss Drew. If you contact the police, your friends will meet a grim fate. This is not a game."

Nancy heard George's cry. "George!" Nancy called into the phone. "George, are you all right?"

"Give her another needle," the voice said. Then, with a clatter, the phone went dead in Nancy's hand.

Nancy slowly pivoted around to face everyone who had been watching her in stunned silence all that time. "Well?" Captain Morita asked.

There was no way she could keep this from the police, Nancy realized, not when the captain was right there. "George and Frank have been kidnapped," she told them breathlessly.

Bess's hands flew to her face. "Oh, no!" she cried. Then she said, "What about Joe?"

"Apparently not," Nancy replied. "I heard two voices, a man's deep one and a raspy one that sounded disguised. I heard George—I think she was drugged."

"What do they want you to do?" Captain Morita asked, whipping out a notebook and pencil from an inside pocket.

"They said they'll call here tomorrow morning at eleven with instructions." Nancy told him the rest of the kidnappers' demands. "They said if I told the police, they'd kill Frank and George."

"Don't worry, Miss Drew, we'll be discreet." The captain began pacing. "It's the money they're after," he said, thinking aloud. "So we'll have to be prepared. I'll take the money to the lab and put a chemical tracer on it. Then we'll repack it in a briefcase and plant a microtransmitter inside. That way, we can nab them after they make the pickup."

"What about me?" Nancy asked. "And Bess and Joe? They want us to leave Hawaii."

"You'll have to leave then," Morita said simply. "After you make the drop-off, I'll handle everything."

"Now, wait just a minute," Nancy said hotly. "You're talking about my two best friends here! I'm not leaving until they're free and the kidnappers are behind bars."

"Young lady, this is a police matter. We don't

need outside interference," Captain Morita said, annoyed.

Just as Nancy was about to respond, Carson spoke up. "My daughter has very good instincts about these things, Captain, and experience as well," he said. "If I were you, I'd treat her as an ally, not a meddling amateur."

"That's right," Bess put in.

Captain Morita was clearly surprised by Nancy's father's comments. He took a deep breath and then cleared his throat too many times. "I'm sure we can find a plan that works for all of us," he finally said. Turning to Nancy, his face still flushed, he asked, "Any suggestions, Ms. Drew?"

"Yes," Nancy said. "What if Bess, Joe, and I board the plane and then get off after it's taxied from the gate? If we could put on airline employee jackets we'd blend in with the crew, wouldn't we? After that we could work undercover on the case."

"I see," said the captain, stone-faced. "Well, let's hope that by then we'll have apprehended the kidnappers. I'm afraid we can't take responsibility for your safety if you choose to become involved."

"I understand, Captain," Nancy said, checking first with Bess, who indicated she was ready for anything. Carson Drew nodded, expressing his confidence. They were behind her.

* * *

Joe sat on the beach and pulled his red-and-black beach towel tighter around his shoulders. He was really going to give it to Frank for making him wait so long. The sun had long since set, and he was still at Makaha Beach.

The only other person still around was Heather Farwell. Since the end of the competition, she'd spent her time swimming and sunning herself. But every so often she had looked over at him and thrown him a big smile.

Joe couldn't understand what Frank saw in Heather—everything about her was so fake.

"What's the matter, Wipeout?" Heather asked in a tone of voice that was all syrup and sugar. She was folding up her beach towel and packing it away. "Did your manager forget about you?"

"He must have," Joe muttered, rubbing the back of his neck. The first thing he was going to do when he got back to his room was throw a couple of quarters in his vibrating bed. After the competition that day every one of his muscles hurt. "Why are you hanging around, Heather? You've got a car, don't you?"

"Sure," Heather answered, "but I thought I'd stay in case you need a lift. You can't walk back to Waikiki from here."

Heather ambled over and put her hands on Joe's shoulders. "You're so tense," she murmured as her fingers gently pushed into his muscles. "Relax."

Joe knew he should tell her to lay off, but the massage felt too good.

"Can I tell you something?" Heather said.

"Sure, why not," Joe said, dropping his head to one side as she continued stroking the back of his neck.

"The real reason I'm here is that Harry asked me to spy on you. He said your real name is Joe Hardy and that you came to Hawaii to make trouble."

Joe put a hand up to stop her. Then he turned to face her. Heather was smiling sweetly.

"Is that so?" Joe said, playing for time.

"He said you think we're thieves or something," she said, her catlike eyes fixed on his. "It's not true, you know."

If Joe hadn't already guessed his cover was blown, he certainly knew it now.

"I think you have us mixed up with somebody else," Heather said with a shrug.

Wouldn't that be a kick in the head, Joe thought. But he didn't say anything.

"Come on," Heather said lightly. "Let me drive you back. It looks like your brother won't be showing up."

He had to admit she was right. Frank must have picked up a hot trail or something. "Okay," he said. "Let's go."

After picking up her handbag and slinging it over her shoulder, Heather led him to her car.

"So tell me more about these so-called crooks I'm supposedly tracking down," Joe asked her, hoping to uncover any detail she might let slip.

"I really don't know much about it," Heather

said smoothly. "Just what I told you. I don't get involved with heavy stuff like that. I have better things to do with my time."

Everything about Heather exuded confidence, Joe thought. "What 'better things'?"

Heather took her eyes away from the road just long enough to give him a sly smile. "Oh, you know," she answered, "I like to swim, and I like to party. I like to get together with people, things like that."

It wasn't what she was saying, it was how she was saying it. Impulsively, Joe leaned toward her and nuzzled her shoulder with his lips.

"That feels good," Heather said, keeping her eyes on the road.

"Hmmmm . . ." Joe said, kissing her neck gently. But as he did, he was reaching into her open handbag. There, a piece of white paper was sticking up like an invitation. When Joe sat back on his side of the car, the note was crumpled tightly in his fist, hidden from Heather.

Pleased with himself, Joe started to enjoy the ride. He had a strong feeling that piece of paper was more than a shopping list.

"Where should I drop you?" Heather asked.

"You can just leave me near the Grand Hawaiian. I have a friend staying there."

"Really? Is she pretty?" Heather asked with a little pout that made Joe want to throw up. "As pretty as me?"

"Actually, she's much prettier," Joe said, smoothly. "But, anyway, thanks for the lift."

Joe stepped into the hotel lobby, to call on Nancy, George, and Bess. If Frank was there, Joe thought, he'd better have a good explanation for hanging him up.

Upstairs, Joe found the door to the girls' suite open, and the sitting room occupied.

"Joe!" Nancy said, rising to meet him. "I'm sorry, but we have bad news." Soon, she'd filled him in.

"By the way," Nancy said gently to a shaken Joe, "this is my dad, Carson Drew, Rachel Maxon, the owner of the hotel, and Captain Morita, who's investigating the murder case."

"Sorry we have to meet under such difficult circumstances," Carson said, extending his hand. Rachel and the captain nodded a greeting.

"Oh, man," Joe moaned, leaning back in the seat he'd taken. If anything had happened to Frank . . .

"Well, I'd better get busy marking the money," the captain said, excusing himself. When he was gone, Joe remembered the note he'd taken from Heather's bag. He pulled it out and smoothed it open. "Want to see something weird? I found this in Heather's handbag."

"Let's see," Bess said, peering over his shoulder. "Nancy, look! The symbols are just like the ones Kame showed us on Niihau!"

Joe handed the paper over to Nancy, who studied it closely. "You're right, Bess," she said. "It's a petroglyph."

Rachel Maxon got up and went over to look,

too. "Those are ancient Hawaiian symbols," she confirmed. "But I can't read them."

"I know someone who can," Nancy said.

Joe was worried. If someone could read those symbols, the same person could also have written them. The only person they knew who could do that was someone Joe didn't think a whole lot of.

Luke Kilauea.

Chapter

Fourteen

"I DON'T TRUST Luke Kilauea!" Joe cried, leaning forward. "I don't care if he can read these symbols or not."

"But, Joe," Bess argued, "this piece of paper may be the only real clue we have. We've got to find out what it means."

"There aren't many people in all of Hawaii who can read those symbols," Rachel pointed out.

"If Nancy knows someone who can interpret the note, I think she should contact that person, Joe," Carson added, keeping his voice level.

Nancy bit her lip and considered what to do. Regretfully, she had to admit that Luke might be working against them. The dead man had a package from Luke's father's lab, didn't he? It was also true that Kame Kilauea was a big man, both in size and reputation.

"Joe, we've got to trust Luke," Nancy said gently. "We need his expertise. Even if he is working against us, we could learn something from him that will lead us to Frank and George."

Running a hand through his thick blond hair, Joe let himself lean back into his chair. "Well, okay," he said, reluctantly. "But I still don't like it."

Nancy dialed Luke's number on Oahu, keeping the phone pressed to her ear. The only sound she heard was unanswered ringing. "Be there," she whispered.

It was no use. "So much for that idea," Nancy said. "He's not there."

"He's probably busy standing guard over Frank," Joe muttered bitterly.

"Joe!" Bess protested.

"I've got to leave, Carson," Rachel murmured.

"Me, too," Nancy's father agreed. He told Nancy to call him if there was anything he could do. As he and Rachel walked out the door, he added, "Hang in there, Joe."

After Carson and Rachel left, the room grew very quiet. Nancy tried Luke's number again, but still there was no answer.

Joe stood up and murmured, "I might as well take off, too. Frank may try to reach me at our place."

To Nancy, that idea seemed like a very slender hope, but she didn't want to say anything to discourage Joe.

"Hey, I have an idea," she said, walking him to the door. "Let's take a drive on the road to Makaha Beach, where Frank and George were headed, tomorrow morning. We can go early, before the kidnappers call. Maybe we'll find something,"

Joe seemed to perk up a bit at that suggestion. He nodded and murmured, "Good thinking, Nan." He waved halfheartedly to Bess and left the room.

"Poor Joe," Bess said after he left.

"Poor Frank," Nancy corrected her. "Poor George. I hope they're okay."

Bess squeezed her eyes shut. "I can't stand to think about George," she blurted out. "Oh, Nancy, what if something really bad happens to her? Or to Frank?"

Bess's bottom lip was quivering, and the rims of her eyes were growing red. It was clear to Nancy that her friend was about to lose it. "It's okay to cry, Bess," Nancy said gently.

"George wouldn't cry," Bess answered. "She'd be too busy figuring out a way to help me! She'd be strong."

"There are different kinds of strong, Bess," Nancy said, walking over and giving her a hug.

That was all Bess needed. Soon tears were pouring down her cheeks. "It's my fault," Bess cried miserably. "I was the one who talked her into coming on this trip."

"Wait a minute," Nancy said, stepping back and holding Bess's hands gently. "I was there. You said, 'Hawaii,' and she said, 'Great.' You didn't exactly twist her arm."

"That's true," Bess said, gulping back another sob.

"Come on," Nancy said, leading her to the bedroom. "We've got to get some rest."

Bess washed up without saying anything more. But when she pulled her blanket down and climbed into bed, Nancy heard her sniff back more tears.

"Bess," Nancy said as she changed into her nightgown, "we're going to find George, and Frank, too. We're going to find them, and we're going to save them."

"Really, Nan?" Bess said, her voice quivering.

"Really," Nancy said, hopping into bed.

"Just hearing you say that makes me feel better," Bess said, sitting up and hugging her knees.

"Let's try to get some rest," Nancy told her. "Tomorrow we'll handle this whole thing."

Bess reached for a tissue and blew her nose. "If you say we'll save them, we will," she said, curling up quietly.

"That's the spirit, Bess," Nancy said.

Giving Bess that assurance made Nancy feel more confident, too. She knew she had to be at her absolute best this time. The people she loved were counting on her. She made her breaths come deep and slow and allowed herself to sleep. Finally, her body obeyed.

The next morning at six, Joe met Nancy and Bess at the hotel. They picked up a few muffins "to go" and set off. Soon they were driving along the road to Makaha Beach, retracing Frank and George's path from the airport. "This is the only road," Bess said, rechecking a map in the back of the Jeep.

"Then they had to be abducted somewhere on it," Nancy said, slowing to just five miles an hour at isolated spots where Frank and George could have been taken. "Joe, you check the right side. Bess, the left," she instructed.

No luck. The stretch of road from the airport to the beach revealed no signs of a struggle. It was nothing but asphalt, wild plants, flowers, and an occasional house.

"Frank and George must have gone without a fight," Joe said, his frustration level rising. "The kidnappers must have taken their car, too."

Bess leaned out the window and gazed at the ocean. "How can something so horrible be happening somewhere so beautiful?"

Up ahead, Nancy saw fields of wildflowers dancing in the bright morning breeze. A flock of small yellow birds, hundreds of them, descended on a grove of banyan trees nearby. "It is gorgeous," Nancy murmured, as the natural beauty washed over her. But it couldn't wash away the pain of her friends' kidnapping.

"Look, it's eight o'clock," she said, glancing at the dashboard. "Maili is not far from here. I think we should see if Luke's home."

"Fine with me," Joe said, his face tightening. "I'd like to find out what he knows, actually."

Doubling back they soon came to Maili. Turning off the main road, Nancy easily found the turquoise-painted house that belonged to Luke's relatives. Luke was outside, tying tomato plants to large stakes with thin strips of cloth. He looked up in surprise when Nancy's Jeep pulled up.

"Aloha," he said, smiling and inviting them to sit at a small table in the garden.

"Luke, we need your help," Nancy explained, filling him in on everything that had happened. "Can you read this?" she asked, handing him the paper Joe had taken out of Heather's bag.

"I recognize some of the symbols but not all," he said, his wide dark eyes searching the page. "This symbol with the crisscross lines means palace. And this one is treasure."

"Treasure palace," Nancy repeated. "That's got to mean an art collection."

Luke put down the paper and shook his head in disgust. "It makes me sick that people would use these symbols to help them in their crimes!"

"Would you just keep reading?" Joe said. There was no missing the hostility in his voice.

"Hey, don't have an attitude with me, man,"

Luke told him. "I did something wrong last time, and you know I'm sorry. I thought we were working together from now on."

"Yeah, Joe," Bess added. "Lighten up. Anybody can make a mistake."

Luke tossed his long hair to the back of his neck, and studied the note again. "Here are numbers, one, two, three. But I've never seen this one, the circles with the dot in the center."

"It looks like a bull's-eye, doesn't it?" Bess asked.

Joe poked his head closer to the note. "Looks like?" he exclaimed. "Those *are* bull's-eyes! This code isn't *all* in native Hawaiian."

"Treasure targets," Nancy murmured. "Palaces one, two, and three. I can't figure out what it means. Can you guys?"

Joe shook his head as Luke and Bess both shrugged.

"Hey," Nancy said, checking her wristwatch. "It's after nine. We'd better get back to the hotel."

"I'm coming with you," Luke said. "I want to help in any way I can." He quickly changed his clothes and stuffed some food in a backpack.

At a quarter to eleven they all raced up to the girls' suite.

Captain Morita was in the room, with two other people. A large electronic device was attached to the phone in the living room of the suite. "Nice of you to show up," he said sarcastically. "This is Nancy Drew, Bess Marvin, and

Joe Hardy. Say hello to Officers Rivera and Jones."

The two officers, a man in his fifties and a woman of about thirty, nodded. Nancy quickly introduced Luke as a good friend who would be helping them out. Morita wasn't pleased, but his full attention was focused on the briefcase on the sofa. "Take a look, but don't touch," he said, pointing at it.

As Nancy and the others peered in, he explained, "Every bill has been treated with a chemical tracer. Between that and the phone tracers and the signaling device we've planted in the case, nabbing these guys should be a piece of cake."

Overconfidence wasn't one of Nancy's favorite characteristics, in herself or in others. "I hope you're right, Captain," she said respectfully. "But if none of—"

The sound of the phone cut Nancy off. A chill shot through her as she glanced at her wrist. It was exactly eleven o'clock. At least the callers were true to their word—so far. Nancy quickly picked up the phone. "Hello?" she said, her throat suddenly dry.

The disguised voice on the other end of the line was creepily familiar. "Nancy?"

"Yes," Nancy said.

"I have your instructions. Listen carefully. You are to bring the item to the Haleakala Volcano, on Maui. Hike into the crater, where you'll come to camping cabin number one. There you'll spend the night tonight. The arrangements have all been taken care of. In the morning, leave the item in the cabin, and go directly to Maui airport and board a plane with your friends to leave Hawaii. When your plane takes off, we'll release your other friends. They are guests of ours for now. No police. Do you understand?"

"I understand," Nancy said.

With a click, the phone went dead.

Captain Morita, who'd been listening on head-phones, let out a gleeful cry. "Great! They're making my life easy. As soon as they try to make the pickup, we descend on them with helicop-ters."

"But we've got to find George and Frank first," Nancy said, cautioning him.

An uneasy feeling came over Nancy as she eyed the officer. In her opinion, Morita was far too ready to burst in and be a hero.

The phone rang again, and Nancy reached for it immediately. "Hello?"

"Police tracer. May I talk to the captain, please?" Nancy dutifully handed the phone to the captain, who listened for a moment.

"A pay phone on Maui, huh?" Morita said. "Thanks."

"That's where the surfing competition goes next," Joe said. "So we know where Willy will be."

"We'll see you on Maui," Morita told them. "A plainclothes cop will be with you after you leave the hotel. Don't look for him—he'll be there. We have officers at all the hotel exits. You should be safe. Good luck."

"Joe and I can go down to buy the tickets," Bess offered.

"Which leaves Luke and me to guard the precious cargo," Nancy said.

After Joe and Bess had gone, Nancy stood gazing out the window, which looked down on the palm-shaded courtyard of the Grand Hawaiian.

Something below caught her eye. A man carrying a briefcase was limping along a side path toward a narrow opening that led to the street.

"Johnny Leong," she said, half under her breath. What was he doing coming out of the hotel he'd been suspended from just the day before? She had to find out.

"Luke, stay here. I've got to go downstairs for a few minutes," she said, already racing out of the room.

When she got to the lobby, Nancy quickly spotted the officer and sneaked around him to the main street outside. It was full of tourists wearing leis and chatting and peering into store windows. Which way had Johnny gone?

Taking a chance, Nancy headed up the boulevard toward the busier section. She kept close to the shops, so she could duck for cover in case Leong turned around. At a traffic light two blocks up, she finally spotted him. He was dangling a set of keys in his hand.

"Johnny!" a woman called, and he spun

around, startled. Nancy was right in his field of vision. Her breath catching, she peered into a bookstore entrance. Then a redheaded boy of about five ran up to the woman. "What, Mommy?" he asked.

"I told you not to run ahead so far," the woman scolded. "Stay with Mommy, okay?"

Nancy breathed a sigh of relief, and watched as Johnny Leong crossed the street, and entered a post office. Her heart pounding, Nancy followed him inside, being as unobtrusive as possible. "Please don't let him turn around," she whispered out loud.

She found a hiding place between two tall women, who were standing in line with parcels. From there, Nancy saw Johnny hurry to a wall of postboxes. Even at a distance she could plainly see the gold numerals over the box: 1119.

Johnny slipped in a key and turned it. Nancy watched as he pulled out a brown package. It had a bright yellow label that she would have known anywhere.

The package was from Kame Kilauea's lab!

Chapter

Fifteen

THOSE MAILERS were supposed to go to a Swiss firm. What was Johnny Leong doing taking them? Nancy wondered. She watched as Johnny opened the briefcase, put the package inside, and snapped the case closed. As he left the post office, walking quickly, Nancy again followed.

Johnny returned to the Grand Hawaiian and entered through the same entrance. But a red light at a pedestrian crossing held Nancy up. The traffic zipped by for what seemed an eternity before she was able to cross. By the time she entered the lobby, Johnny had disappeared.

She was frustrated that she'd lost him. Just then a familiar voice coming up behind her said, "There you are, Nancy." Carson walked up terribly distraught. "Well, what's happening?" he demanded. "Did the kidnappers call?"

In all the confusion Nancy had neglected to keep her father informed. After apologizing, Nancy explained, finishing with, "Luke's upstairs, and Bess and Joe are getting our tickets."

"Come on. I'll go back up with you," Carson said. Inside the elevator he let out a kind of little grunt that told Nancy he was far from happy.

"Try not to worry about me, okay?" Nancy said, pressing the button for the fourth floor. "It's going to be all right."

Carson nodded slowly. "You've been saying that since you were four years old," he said affectionately. "You don't seem to understand that I have perfect faith in you. It's the bad guys I have no confidence in."

Then he said something which took Nancy by surprise. "I'm worried about Rachel, too," he admitted suddenly. "Something's wrong, and I don't know what it is."

The elevator opened onto the fourth floor, and they got out. "What makes you say that, Dad?" Nancy asked.

"As I was going over her accounts, I noticed a large infusion of cash came into the hotel about two months ago. When I asked Rachel about it, she told me she'd had to take on a silent partner."

"But I thought she was totally committed to keeping control of the hotel herself," Nancy said.

"Me, too. I guess she needed the cash so badly, she had to compromise. According to her, the silent partner only owns a minority share—around twenty-five percent, she claims. But there's something else. She wouldn't tell me who the partner was."

"Why not?" Nancy asked.

"Apparently, that was part of the deal she made. The silent partner was to remain anonymous. In any event, I'm sure it's not a big corporation. Rachel would never let them in the door."

"I hope not," Nancy said somberly. "I wonder who the silent partner could be—"

"That by itself wouldn't worry me," Carson went on as they approached Nancy's room. "It's her uncertainty. Every time I recommend something, she has to check with this so-called minority partner first. I'm afraid she may have sold off more of the hotel than she's admitting. I sense that she's not telling me everything." Sighing, he gave her an unhappy smile. "Well, never mind. I'll take care of Rachel as best I can. You take care of yourself and the others, okay? Don't forget—call me, keep me informed."

"I will, Dad," Nancy promised, waving goodbye. Opening the door to her suite, she was relieved to find Luke still there, sitting on the couch beside the briefcase.

Bess came in from the bedroom, toting her fuchsia canvas overnight bag, which was bulging with clothes. "I'm all set," she announced. "Joe's grabbing a sandwich. He'll be up in a minute."

Nancy sat down on the chair across from Luke.

There were things she had to know from him, and she had to ask carefully. "Luke, is there anything else that your father sends here to Oahu other than the flowers?"

"Only cuttings of plants with healing properties," Luke replied.

"Hmm." Nancy was puzzled. Why would Johnny Leong be picking up packages of plants? It wasn't as if he worked for Futurehealth of Zurich. Also, why was he hanging around the Grand Hawaiian when he'd been told to get off the premises? As far as Nancy could see, Rachel Maxon's hotel figured into some of these shady dealings.

Joe burst in then, the remains of a sandwich in his hand. "Okay," he said. "Let's get going. I want to stop at my place and pick up a few things first."

Nancy tossed some clothes in her bag, and they left. "Nancy," Joe whispered in the hallway, "wait till I tell you what I just heard." He eyed Luke suspiciously. "I'll tell you later," he said.

Only after they were at the Economy Inn did he draw her aside. "When I was at the sandwich bar, I overheard Harry Leong, talking to some guy in a suit. He said something about his *brother* Johnny!"

"So Johnny Leong *is* related to Harry," Nancy said, nodding slowly. "There seem to be more and more intriguing connections around here," she said, and told Joe about tailing Johnny Leong.

"Yeah, so what does it all add up to?" Joe said.

"That I can't say, Joe," she answered, "but I hope we'll find out on Maui."

At the airport they had to hustle to catch the fifty-seater they were taking to Maui.

"Nan!" Bess exclaimed when they stepped on board. "Look who's on our flight. Hello, Willy."

Willy seemed stunned when he saw them enter, but he covered with a wide grin. "Cool," he said as they sat down across from him. "Wipeout, man, how're you doing? Going to surf in Maui, huh? Give it one more try? Ha-ha."

"How have you been, Willy?" Bess asked sweetly as she slid into the seat next to his.

"Everything's cool," he replied with a noncommittal shrug.

"Where are you staying on Maui?" she asked.

"Just a regular, you know, motel," he answered. "How about you?"

"Oh, same kind of thing," Bess said, shrugging him off. Good old Bess, Nancy thought from across the aisle. Bess was trying to get information out of him without revealing any of hers. Unfortunately, Willy seemed to be doing the same to her.

"That must be the Haleakala National Park," Joe said, pressing toward the window. Nancy leaned over and looked out, too. Below, touching the clouds, was a high, flat mountaintop, with an enormous crater.

"That crater goes on for miles," Nancy said in awe. "I read that you could fit the whole island of Manhattan in there!"

When the plane landed, Willy turned to Bess and smiled. "Have a good time on Maui."

"Where are you going now?" Bess asked in her most charming voice. "Can we give you a lift in our cab?"

"Thanks, but I'm going to rent a motorbike," he replied. With a flirtatious wink to Bess and a wave to the rest of them, he went off.

"Bess and Joe, rent a car and follow him," Nancy suggested. "The thieves didn't say if you were to go with me. We'll assume you're not to. Willy might lead you to Frank and George, although I wouldn't bet on it. I'll take Luke with me, though, okay?"

Joe was dubious but finally said, "I guess that's okay." Nancy reminded him that a plainclothes cop was supposed to be guarding her and the money, although none of them had spotted him yet. "Okay, we're out of here," Joe said, and took Bess's arm, heading them toward the car rental counter.

"I guess we'll see you back here at the airport tomorrow morning," Bess said to Nancy and Luke. "Take care of yourselves, you two!"

"We will," Nancy said, hugging Bess and Joe goodbye before she headed outside with Luke to hail a cab.

"We're going to the crater," she told the driver, a woman of about fifty with salt and pepper hair worn in braids.

"It's going to cost you," the driver cautioned.

"That's okay," Nancy said, climbing in with Luke.

They started climbing up into the hills, every mile taking them higher. Out one window was the ocean, deep blue and calm, ringed with sandy beaches that stretched forever. On the other side of them was lush mountain greenery. "This is some climb," Nancy said as she felt her ears pop.

"Wait, you're going to be above the clouds soon," the driver called from the front. "Haleakala is over ten thousand feet high."

The vegetation around them changed as they climbed higher. The ocean fell out of view behind a layer of mist, and panoramic mountaintops came into sight.

"I'm putting on a sweatshirt," Nancy said, as cool air slipped into the cab.

Luke remained silent, his eyes riveted on the view. Nancy reached in her bag and got out a rolled-up blue sweatshirt. Zipping it, Nancy gazed out the window. "Truly awesome," she said as the mist and clouds parted below and above them. "It's as if we're riding in the sky," she said.

"You are in the House of the Sun," Luke said, "Pele's holiest place. In this place, the demigod Maui, son of Hina, snared the Sun. He made the Sun promise to cross the sky more slowly to give the crops more time to grow, and fishermen more time to fish, and his mother's tapa cloth more time to dry. The Sun is careful now to cross the sky slowly in Haleakala, House of the Sun."

"I can see why your ancestors would worship here," Nancy said, impressed. "It's so beautiful!" She turned to look out the other window, and saw several Hawaiian Islands in the distance.

"There is the Big Island," Luke said, pointing to the island of Hawaii. "The tall volcano on the Big Island is Mauna Kea, and behind it Mauna Loa and Kilauea, my namesake. Pele makes her home there, now that the other volcanoes are extinct."

Nancy was so fascinated by Luke's stories about Hawaii that she scarcely noticed when the cab pulled to a stop at the trailhead. There, they paid the driver and got out to descend into the crater itself, picking their way carefully down the steep path. Nancy wondered briefly where Morita and his plainclothesmen were. He said he'd see them on Maui. This was the perfect spot to be highjacked and Nancy wanted to know Morita was close by.

Winding down the rough trail, Nancy and Luke entered the silent, eerie world inside the extinct crater. Luke pointed to a silvery, spiky plant that seemed to grow everywhere. "It's very rare," he told Nancy. "The silversword plant grows only here in this crater, and even here it is endangered by plants brought in from abroad. My father is doing research with it to help it survive." He bent down and collected some seeds.

"It seems like everything's endangered," Nancy commented. "The native plants and animals,

Rachel's hotel, Frank and George . . ." Her voice trailed off to a whisper, lost in the vastness of the darkening crater.

"The sun's going down," Luke said. "We'd better hurry. Cabin number one is still a ways off."

They got there just before dark, using their flashlights to light up the trail. The silence was eerie, with only the whipping wind above to punctuate it. Nancy was hoping Morita was near.

"The kidnapper said that everything would be arranged for us," Nancy said with a shiver, when they spotted the small rustic cabin marked with a painted One. She opened the door and they went inside. "Hello?" Nancy called into the two-room structure. No one was there.

Luke slipped off his backpack and took out a large papaya, a block of cheese, and a knife. Nancy opened up her bag and pulled out the box of crackers Bess had bought that morning.

"There's kindling for a fire," Luke said, walking over to the small stone fireplace. "Later I'll replace it." He laid a fire and struck a match to it to take the chill out of the cabin.

By the time the fire was crackling, Nancy had sliced the papaya and cheese. "Here, Luke," she said, offering it to him.

"So here we are," Luke said with a smile as he ate. "Do you think they'll come for their money tonight?"

"No," Nancy said. "I think they'll come and take it after we're gone. Why let us know who they are when they can stay anonymous?" She sighed and picked up the briefcase from the crude chair where Luke had put it. "Let's just check it one more time, okay," she said.

Nancy flipped the snaps. The lid flew open. She could hardly believe what she saw inside. Instead of the neatly wrapped bundle of bills, there— bound in rubber bands—was a thick wad of blank, white paper!

"The money!" she gasped in horror. "Luke, the money is gone!"

Chapter

Sixteen

I CAN'T UNDERSTAND IT," Luke gasped, staring at the blank paper. "How—"

"Are you sure you were with the money the whole time?" Nancy pressed him. "Every second?"

"Of course!" Luke insisted. Then he hesitated. "Except . . ." His mouth opened slightly and stared beyond Nancy with a pained expression.

"You did leave it for a minute, didn't you?" Nancy said, shaken. Then she drew a deep breath and faced him squarely. "Okay, Luke, you've got to tell me what happened. And don't leave anything out."

"All right," Luke said, obviously distressed.

"Let's see, you left, and after about two or three minutes, there was a knock at the door. I looked through the peephole and saw a girl. She said please, could someone help her. Her door was stuck, and if she couldn't open it, she was going to miss her plane. She seemed nice, and I felt sorry for her. It took a few minutes to get to her room around the corner and jiggle the door open. When I finished she thanked me, and I went back to your room. The briefcase was still there, exactly the way I'd left it."

"Did you check to see if the money was still inside?" Nancy asked.

"Well, no," Luke confessed. "I mean, nothing looked like it had been moved or anything." He sat down on a bench, and put his head in his hands. "How could I have been so stupid?"

Nancy tried not to show her disapproval. "Luke," she said, "what did the girl look like?"

"Thin, tall, with dark hair," Luke said, staring at the crude wooden floor.

"Heather," Nancy said through gritted teeth. "Of course. She distracted you while someone else made the switch. They must have been watching us almost from the time I found the money."

Luke let out a sorry sigh. "I know I let you down in a big way. I let myself down, too."

At least Luke didn't shy away from taking responsibility when he messed up. Nancy really liked that about him.

"It's okay, Luke," she said quietly. "Obviously, this was all part of their plan. They set us up, and we were dumb enough to fall for it. All of us, the police, too—not just you," she finished.

"Well," Luke said, raising his head. "What do we do now?"

"I guess," Nancy said, "we just follow through with our instructions. Frank and George are depending on us. Anyway, it's too dangerous to hike out of here in the dark. I just wish I knew where Morita and his men are. I'd have thought they'd have contacted us by now."

"Do you feel safe here?" Luke asked, staring out at the night sky.

"Perfectly," Nancy replied. "This is the last place in the world the crooks are going to show up. That," she added, lying down on a bottom bunk, "was their whole point—to get rid of us."

By the time the sun rose over the spectacular rim of the crater, Nancy and Luke had left the cabin with the case inside. From there, they hiked back to the Visitors' Center at the summit and got a cab for the airport.

When they arrived at the terminal, there was still no Morita. Where could he and his men be? Nancy called Honolulu and left a message for him. Then they met Joe and Bess, who told them that Willy had given them the slip.

"He must have known we were tailing him," Bess said.

"Listen," Nancy said, "all we can do now is follow our plan. We have to get on that plane and hope they release Frank and George as promised. If not, we'll find them after we sneak off."

"Let's do what we came here to do," Joe agreed, and led the way to their plane.

The pilot, a man of about forty, met them at the door and led them into the cockpit, where they could talk privately. "Captain Morita has been in touch with us. His plainclothesmen got hung up, and he'll tell you what happened later. We're all set to do what he asked," he told them. "There are flight suits that our crew wears hanging in the rear closet. You can go back there and slip them on over your clothes. We'll taxi to the end of the runway, where you'll hop out. Good luck," the man said.

After stepping into their flight suits, they sat. With time to kill, Luke took out the coded note and started going over it again.

"This glyph, here," Luke said, pointing to a long, thin one with a squiggly line coming out of it. "I think it's the symbol for unity. See, the needle is for sewing things together—"

Suddenly Luke slapped his knee. "The needle —that's it! Of course. How could I have been so blind? The Iao Valley needle! It's a well-known landmark not far from here. A tall, thin rock formation covered with moss."

"What about this next symbol?" Bess wondered. "What could it mean?"

"These are all numbers, that's what gets me," Luke said, pointing them out. "2, 10, 17, 25, 26, 27 . . ."

All at once Joe snapped his fingers. "Hey, what if those are the dates of their heists? There were robberies on the second, tenth, and seventeenth. And the twenty-fifth was the night we ambushed them at the mausoleum."

"Good thinking, Joe," Nancy cried. "Now we're getting somewhere."

"Thanks to Luke," Joe said, giving his new friend a quick smile.

"Well, I guess I'm good for something," Luke said modestly.

"Hmm," Nancy said. "The twenty-sixth was yesterday. I wonder if any place on Maui got hit last night?" She walked to a magazine rack and pulled out a copy of the morning paper. "Here it is. Look at this, guys—'Hale Hoikeike, the museum off Iao Valley Road, was burglarized last night. Numerous objects were taken, most of them priceless native Hawaiian totems, valued at over four hundred thousand dollars. The police have no leads as to . . .' "

"We're too late for that one," Joe said. "But what about the twenty-seventh? That's tonight!"

Luke studied the glyph in front of the number 27. "It means 'maiden,' " he said. " 'Young girl.' " He frowned, concentrating, then burst out, "The marble statue of the maiden shrine, out past the town of Hana!"

"That's it!" Joe exclaimed. "The next place they're going to hit."

"Great!" Nancy said. "Now all we have to do is get out to Hana before the crooks do. We'll stake it out then follow them. We can capture them and demand they tell us where Frank and George are."

"Er, excuse me," came a deep male voice, startling them all. "But I believe we've reached your destination." It was a flight attendant.

They'd been so busy talking that they hadn't realized that the plane had stopped taxiing. "Whoops," Nancy said with a laugh.

At about that same moment Frank Hardy's eyes fluttered open and a stabbing pain shot through his head. Whatever his kidnappers had given him to make him sleep hadn't agreed with him.

His vision was blurred. "Whew," he said with a shake of his head that only made the pain worse. He looked down and saw that his ankles were tied together.

He could feel that his wrists were bound, too, behind his back. In fact, a short struggle revealed that he was tied to the chair he was sitting in. Pressing backward, he felt the warmth of another person. Soft hair brushed against the back of his neck. George, he realized.

His eyes were focusing better now, and he could see that they were in a softly lit room that was painted a warm peach color. A white laminate shelf ran around the entire room. On the shelf were art objects, dozens of them. Many were made of intricate gold filigree or carved brass. On the walls, several large canvases hung. Frank recognized one as being painted by Monet, a famous French impressionist.

"George," Frank said quietly. There was no response. "Nice of them to give us accommodations with so much class, huh?" he said, trying again.

"Oooohhh . . ." George moaned, coming to.

At least she's alive, Frank thought. He hoped she was feeling better than he had when he first came to.

"George, it's me, Frank," he whispered to her. "Are you all right?"

"I—I think so," came the faint reply. "Where are we, Frank?"

"I'm not sure," he replied. He thought back to the last thing he could remember—the gun pointing at him and then the soft *ping*. A tranquilizer gun, he realized now. They'd been kidnapped, not murdered. But why?

Then he had a vague recollection of coming to briefly and hearing the sounds of a boat at sea. A man's voice had said, "He's coming around. Give him another injection." It was enough for Frank to assume that they'd been taken to another island by boat.

"Are you thinking what I'm thinking?" Frank asked softly. "That we've got to get out of here?"

"I feel sick," George moaned. "And I can't move. How are we going to escape?"

Just then footsteps moving toward the room alerted them that someone was about to enter. When the door was flung open, Frank found himself staring up at an old man with a long sparse beard. He shuffled toward Frank.

"Well, now," said the old man, "I see that you've had a good rest and you're awake and alert. Good. I assure you both that as soon as the conditions of your ransom are met, you'll be released unharmed."

Frank couldn't see George's face, but he could feel her body relax. As for himself, he didn't believe a word of it. Kidnappers didn't let you see their faces unless they meant to kill you.

At that moment, things took a different turn, though. The door opened, and in walked two very unfriendly-looking men. One wore casual clothing, a T-shirt and jeans, and the other had on a tan business suit with highly polished tan shoes. Frank felt George flinch as they entered.

"The money's all counted. It's over a million," the one wearing jeans said.

The businessman added, "But we had a problem at the airport. Those kids didn't leave Hawaii. They got on the plane and then got off again at the end of the runway. Rico's tailing them now."

The old man's face darkened. "I see," he said. "I see. Tsk, tsk, tsk. The big man isn't going to like this—not one bit." He stared at Frank and

George, and his eyes narrowed. "I'm afraid this changes everything," he said calmly. "It's too bad for you that your friends are unable to follow instructions. As it is, we'll have to take care of you in a different way from what we'd planned. But first," he said, "first we'll take care of your friends."

Chapter

Seventeen

FRANK WISHED he could stand up and knock heads together. As far as he was concerned, these jerks were several steps lower than slime.

"Wait a minute," George said, pleading. "What are you going to do to them?"

"Never mind," said the old man, stroking his beard. "You cannot help them now. If you are overexcited we can give you another injection . . ."

"No!" George said. "No more injections. I'll be quiet."

The old man chuckled, nodding at George. "A wise decision," he said. With a wave of his hand, he signaled his henchmen to leave. Giving Frank and George a final creepy smile, he slammed the door shut behind him. Frank listened as voices in the next room rose in heated conversation for a few moments. Then an outside door opened and closed, followed by the sounds of people getting into a car and driving off. Then there was silence.

"Now's our chance, George," he said urgently. "We've got to get out of here."

"Sounds good to me," George whispered back. "But how? I don't know about you, but I'm tied up pretty tight."

Frank scanned the room for something that could cut rope. "What a lovely crystal vase that is, the one by the window. How about if we smash it. That should give us shards sharp enough to cut with."

"Frank, I don't want to discourage you, but that vase is a good fifteen feet away," George said. "The way my ankles are tied, I'm not going anywhere."

"Hmm," Frank murmured, mulling over their situation. "We can bunny hop!" he said suddenly.

"Bunny hop?"

"It's easy—just one, two, three, and hop," Frank explained.

"Frank, you're losing it," George said.

"Come on, George, let's give it a try. One, two, three, hop!"

On the "hop" they used all their strength to

rise from their chairs and push—Frank forward and George backward. "Great!" Frank cried jubilantly. "We moved a good six inches!"

With many more exhausting hops, the two reached the window, where Frank managed to knock the crystal vase to the floor with his head.

"Now comes the hard part," Frank said. "First we'll hop back to where the floor is clear. Then we've got to tilt and fall over so I can reach the glass."

On "three" they managed to tip their chairs over, and Frank snatched up a thick piece of crystal.

"Careful, now," George said. "Don't slit my wrists, okay? I haven't given up hope of living through this."

The sharp glass did its work, and slowly the ropes began to fray.

"Something just occurred to me," George said as Frank worked. "What if they come back while we're on the floor like this? They'll kill us on the spot."

"True," Frank replied. "But let's not think about that right now."

Two minutes later George was free. Once the pins and needles in her hands subsided, she was able to cut Frank free, too. Carefully they tiptoed to the door and tried it.

It opened up into a long hallway lined with doors. To the far end was a living room, which was empty. They headed for it. The room was large, with plush white sofas and a huge fireplace. "Our kidnappers certainly have good taste," Frank said sarcastically. "Check out the fine art—oil paintings, native masks. Lots of these things I recognize from pictures Mr. Watanabe gave us."

"Frank, one thing bothers me," George said. "Why would they leave us here alone? For a bunch of smart crooks, it seems a stupid thing to do."

Frank shrugged. "Seems that way, but maybe it was an emergency. Maybe they didn't know who they were dealing with," he added, grinning. "Let's get out of here."

They ran for the front door, and Frank extended his hand for the knob. Before he could grab it, the door flew open. There, blocking their exit, was the man in the tan suit, pointing a semiautomatic pistol at Frank's face.

Behind him came the old man and the other thug. "Going so soon?" the gang leader said, giving them a cruel smile. "I wouldn't hear of it. Sit down, both of you. I insist."

Frank and George were led to a couch and forced to sit. The old man sat opposite them in an armchair, and the other two stood behind the couch. Frank could feel the barrel of a gun nuzzling the back of his head.

"This behavior is really very rude," the old man scolded. "We've shown you the best hospitality, and you have rewarded us by breaking a priceless antique. Bad behavior like that, my dear children, must be punished."

"Can you believe this view?" Bess said, as they chugged up the mountainside on the narrow, potholed road to Hana. Fields of brightly colored flowers swayed in the breeze as a herd of cattle lazily munched the thick grass under their feet. As they climbed higher up the cliffside, sheer rocky drops fell off below them. The road became almost too narrow for another car to pass in the opposite direction.

"If a truck comes down the mountain, we're done for," Bess said, laughing, but Nancy knew that her friend really was worried.

"How far to Hana?" Nancy asked.

"Only another ten miles or so," Luke said. "But that's as the crow flies. As the road goes, twenty or thirty. The shrine with the statue of the maiden is another fifteen miles beyond."

Their rented car bounced like crazy every time it hit a pothole. Joe was at the wheel, and he kept apologizing, even though he wasn't going very fast.

"If I'd have known how rough this road was, I'd have rented a Jeep," he muttered.

"This car doesn't have any pickup either," he complained. After another mile or two, they were going so slowly that every car passed them. "Gee, I can't win on this road, can I?"

"Not the way some people drive," Luke commented. "See what I mean? Look at this guy behind us."

Nancy turned to peer through the rear window. A black sedan was approaching faster and faster. It never blew its horn, though.

Nancy waved at the driver, hoping to catch his attention. The man behind the wheel ignored her. His face was pockmarked and looked familiar, though Nancy couldn't place it. "Hey," she said, suddenly worried. "Something strange is going on here."

As she spoke, they came to a bend in the road that dropped hundreds of feet below them on the left. The car behind them picked that exact moment to pass illegally—on the right. "Look out, Joe!" Nancy cried, alerting him just in time. Joe had to swerve to the left to avoid a collision. He swung their car into the oncoming lane.

The sedan did not go past them. It drew alongside, and its driver swung to the left, ramming their car and sending it toward the guard rail. *Bang!* It hit the rail once. *Bang! Bang!* Twice more, and still the sedan forced them into the rail.

"Joe, look out!" Nancy shouted. "There's no guard rail up ahead!"

BANG! With a screech of metal, the sedan hit them one last time before Joe lost control of the vehicle. Skidding, the car fishtailed toward the unprotected cliff edge!

Bess screamed at the top of her lungs, but was almost drowned out by Luke's bloodcurdling yell.

The left rear tire gave out a loud pop as the car swerved backward dangerously close to the edge. "Nancy! We're going over the cliff!" Joe shouted.

Chapter

Eighteen

NANCY PREPARED HERSELF for the long fall to her death on the rocks below—then dramatically the world stopped moving and spinning. Everything stood still, as in a cartoon when a character runs past the edge of the cliff, then hangs in midair until he realizes where he is.

Miraculously their fall never came. The car had slid backward halfway off the cliff and was balanced perfectly like a seesaw. "We must have caught on something," Nancy said to her stunned companions.

Not daring to open her door in case she tipped the precarious balance, she peered out the side window.

"We have to climb out my window one by

one," she told them. "Don't open a door. I'll go first, in case there are other problems."

Slinging her handbag over her neck, she grabbed the top of her open window and pulled herself out of the car.

"Okay, be careful how you move," Nancy called in to the others. Joe let Bess go next. Her blue eyes were wide with panic as she crawled over the front seat. When she moved to the front, the car shifted and bounced slightly. "Don't panic, whatever you do," Nancy warned her friend. "Just reach your hand out to me."

"I'm afraid it will go over!" Bess said. She was clinging to the window frame for dear life.

"You've got to," Nancy said calmly but firmly. "Do it, Bess—now. I don't know how much longer the car will stay balanced."

Scrunching her eyes shut, Bess started inching herself out the window.

"Okay, I've got you," Nancy said, taking her arms. "Slowly, slowly, okay, come on, come on— There!" Bess slid onto the ground, sobbing. "Next," Nancy called.

From inside the car, she heard Joe and Luke arguing that the other should go first. "Come on, you guys!" Nancy yelled. "This car can plunge to the bottom at any moment!"

That was enough for Luke. He scrambled deftly out the window. "Easy now, Joe. The balance is really tricky," she called to him.

As Joe was halfway out the window, the car, lighter now, began to seesaw. With each swing, it came closer to sliding off the cliff. "Joe, quick!" Nancy shouted. "It's slipping!"

Joe scrambled as best he could, but the car was swaying violently now. Nancy heard the scrape of metal as the axle slid off its mooring. "Jump for it!" Luke screamed as the car swayed one last time and dropped.

Joe lunged as the car was going over the edge of the cliff. Luke jumped forward and caught Joe's forearm. He leapt so far that his waist was at the cliff edge, but he didn't loosen his grip on Joe, who was now dangling in midair. Nancy dove for Luke's legs, hauling him backward. Slowly both boys were back on land, safe and gulping in deep lungfuls of air. They were all alive!

Shakily Nancy crawled over and stared down into the precipice. Two hundred feet below, shattered on rocks, their car was smoking, the flames being doused by pounding surf. Suppressing a shiver, she slid back to where her friends were sitting.

"Well, Luke," Joe said, patting him on the back. "I guess you're not one of them after all. Sorry I misjudged you."

"That's okay," Luke said, smiling. "Right now, I'm just glad to be alive. It sure does take a lot to convince you," he teased.

"You can say that again," Bess echoed. "Boy, if I ever get my hands on the guy who ran us off the road . . ."

"Did you get a look at the license plate, Nan?" Joe asked, brushing off his jeans.

"No," Nancy replied. "But I did see the driver. He was big and mean looking, with a pock-marked face. Ring a bell, anybody?"

The others all shook their heads. "Now what do we do?" Luke asked. "We have no wheels. Do we walk on into Hana or turn back?"

"If we hitch back to the nearest town, we can report this to the police, rent another car, and still get out to Hana before dark," Joe said.

"I think it would save time if we reported everything to Captain Morita instead," Nancy said. "The local police might detain us and we'd lose time. And by now we can hope he's had word of Frank and George. Maybe they've been released."

"Sounds like a good plan to me," Luke said as Nancy got up and waved down a passing pickup truck.

The driver was glad to help them, and a few minutes later they arrived at a small town outside of Hana. Joe called Mr. Watanabe, and Luke went to get another car. Nancy and Bess placed another call to Captain Morita in Honolulu.

Morita apologized that the plainclothesmen he'd assigned to guard them and the money missed the plane in Honolulu. Then after they did get another plane to Maui, their rental car nearly blew up on the road to Haleakala Volcano. So, Nancy realized, she and her friends had had no police protection at all. She was glad she hadn't known.

After apologizing, Morita immediately became belligerent, acting as if all the glitches with the police were somehow Nancy's fault. "You're to get off this case at once and stay off it, do you understand?" he demanded. "It's too dangerous. You just forget about this case!"

Nancy was undeterred. "Captain," she said patiently, "my friends are still being held. I can't just forget about them."

"I haven't forgotten them, either," the captain said angrily. "But at this point all we can do is wait for the chemical tracer on the money to show up. The money should lead us to your friends eventually."

Eventually, thought Nancy. Frank and George could be dead by then.

"Captain," Nancy said suddenly, "we have good reason to believe that thieves who may be connected to the kidnapping plan to make a heist tonight. I think they're going to try to steal the marble statue of the maiden at the shrine near Hana. We're going to stake out the shrine and then follow them. Hopefully, they'll confess where Frank and George are being held."

"Now, listen to me," the captain said, cutting her off. "You're to stay put. I'll catch the next plane to Maui, and my people and I will stake out that shrine tonight. I'll call you first thing in the morning to tell you what happened. But I repeat," the captain finished emphatically, "you are to stay off this case. Get a hotel room and tell the local police where you are. Is that clear?" Morita asked.

"I hear you," Nancy said, wishing she'd never revealed their plans to him.

The grim truth was that Frank and George had not been released and were still in danger. The thieves must have seen Nancy and the others sneak off the plane. Nancy pounded the phone in frustration. Maybe if she got some rest, she might be able to place the face of the driver who tried to run them off the road. She'd seen him before; she knew she had. But where?

The old man stared intently into Frank's eyes. "You made a mistake trying to escape," he said. "But it does not matter. The big man has no further use for you." Then he turned to George. "He wants to hold on to the young lady awhile longer, in case we should need a hostage in an emergency."

Frank glanced over at George. If she was scared, she gave no sign of it. Her face reflected icy hatred.

At that moment the front door opened, and a huge man with a pockmarked face came in. "I took care of that business over on Maui," he told the old man with a sickly smile.

"Thank you, Rico. The big man will be pleased," the old man replied. He turned back to Frank and George. "Your friends, I'm afraid, had a fatal accident earlier today."

Frank heard George's strangled cry and found it hard not to cry out himself. No! he said to himself. Don't panic—stay cool. Maybe they're just saying that to scare us. But the huge man's face gave no hint that he was lying.

"Rico," the old man said, "tie Mr. Hardy up again. I think he'd like to see our beautiful river."

Rico went for a length of rope. When he returned, he bound Frank's wrists and ankles tightly.

"Jonathan, help Rico," the old man said to the man in the suit.

"Hang in there, George," Frank called to her as they dragged him out the door. They threw him in the back of a sedan and started up a bumpy road. Frank was lying on his back, staring out the back window at a strange orange glow that lit up the darkening sky. By the time the car stopped, it was totally dark, except for the eerie orange glow. Frank wondered if there was a forest fire nearby, but there was no smell of burning wood.

"All out," Rico commanded. He and the other thug opened the back door and dragged Frank out and began carrying him down a jungle trail. Soon the sound of rushing water filtered through the underbrush. The thugs dropped Frank onto the ground at the water's edge. Rico pulled an air raft out of the bag he was carrying and blew it up. Jonathan brushed dirt from his shiny tan shoes.

Huffing, Rico half-filled the raft with air and laid Frank into it.

"Bye-bye," Jonathan murmured, pushing the raft into the water. Frank gritted his teeth and struggled against the ropes. All he got for his efforts were rope burns.

Shivering as the water soaked his clothes, Frank wondered why they hadn't just thrown him in the water to drown.

Then a roar up ahead told him why. They hadn't needed to. A waterfall would do their work for them. Tying his arms and legs was just to scare Frank so he'd have no control as he met the raging waterfall head on!

Approaching the falls, Frank tried to brace himself. Suddenly, though, the world gave way beneath him, and his own screams were lost in the roaring of the falls.

Chapter

Nineteen

TUMBLING OVER AND OVER, Frank had the breath knocked out of him. Water forced its way up his nose and into his mouth as his head was tossed under the black foam.

He was too stunned to react when he finally reached the bottom, but a jolt from a rock brought him back to consciousness, and his body cried for air.

Desperately he flapped his bound legs as if they were a fishtail. He did manage to get to the surface for one giant gulp of air, but he wasn't going to last long doing that.

Sinking again, Frank hit some sharp stones on the river bottom. A jagged rock, needle sharp and pointy, jutting straight up scraped his arm. As the pain from the wound traveled to his brain, so did an idea. If he could manage to wedge that stone into the knotted rope around his wrists . . .

More desperate kicking brought him to the surface for more air. Opening his mouth as wide as he could, he took in as much as his lungs could hold. Then he sank again, this time aiming for the sharp rock.

Frank did manage to jam the tip of the rock into the knot. Working his arms up and down, he kept at it until the rock forced the rope to loosen. Luckily his hands had been tied in front of him, so he could bring the rope to his teeth and work on the knot some more.

Success! The knot fell away and he could get his hands free. Stroking up, he burst out of the water and gasped wildly.

It didn't take long to undo the knots on his ankles. His aunt Gertrude could have made better ones than Rico and his pal Jonathan had, Frank thought contemptuously.

He swam the twenty yards to shore, pulled himself out of the water, and collapsed on the ground, still gasping. Looking over at the rushing water, he realized how lucky he had been not to have been killed by the falls. The air raft must have protected him a bit.

Shivering in the chill night air, Frank saw that it was pitch dark now. The moon, if there was one, couldn't penetrate the lush jungle canopy overhead. He had to be realistic. There was no way he was going to find his way back to the road at night. Even if he knew the way, he'd be too exhausted to make it.

"Cheer up," Frank told himself. "You love camping, remember?" He'd just have to forget about the gnawing hunger in his belly, the aches of his battered body, and the icy chill of wearing damp clothes, and he'd be fine.

Above him an owl hooted. At least he had some company. He just hoped any other visitor the night brought would be as friendly. Reaching out, he plucked a few broad leaves from a thick tapa plant and carried them to the base of a banyan tree. He covered his shivering body with them. The leaves were a lot more effective than he'd thought they'd be.

"Good night, buddy," he called to the owl. "Don't let me sleep too late in the morning, okay? I have a few things to take care of."

The sky was just beginning to lighten outside the window of the Keanea Inn, the small hotel outside Hana, when a jangling phone got Nancy out of bed. "Hello?" she said sleepily.

"Captain Morita here," came the officer's voice. "I thought you might like to know that we captured two suspects trying to steal the statue of the maiden last night."

"Great!" Nancy said excitedly. "You mean, they're in custody?"

"You got it," said the captain. "Right now we're at police headquarters in Kahului, where they're being questioned."

"What about Frank and George?" Nancy asked. "Are the two cases involved? Were you able to locate them?"

The phone was silent for a moment longer than Nancy could stand. "You did follow the thieves to their hideout before you took them in last night—didn't you?" she said.

"How could I? I had to arrest them," Morita said defensively. "If we'd let them take the statue all the way off its pedestal, it might have gotten damaged."

"What about my friends, Captain?" Nancy demanded. "They're your primary responsibility. They're your case."

"Quit worrying, will you?" The captain seemed annoyed now. "We'll find your friends—by tracing the money or through these thieves."

Nancy didn't take much comfort in that.

"Who were the thieves, by the way?" Nancy asked.

"A good-looking girl by the name of Heather Farwell and some clown called Harry Leong," Morita said.

"I can tell you who they work with, if you want to know," Nancy said. "Willy Brannigan."

"Thanks," Morita said dismissively. "Look, I've got to go. Don't worry. We're still working on the kidnapping. What we have to do now is connect these two cases."

Nancy told herself that losing her temper wouldn't win her any brownie points. "Captain, I'd like to come to Kahului with my friends and talk to Heather and Harry. They might know where Frank and George are. I'm sure they do."

"Permission denied," Morita said quickly. "Now, be smart, and go back to Honolulu and wait for word. Goodbye." Before she could say anything else he hung up. Nancy slammed the phone into its cradle, fuming.

"Bess, wake up," Nancy said, shaking her sleeping friend. "Captain Morita caught Heather and Harry last night. Meet me in Joe's room." Nancy quickly got dressed, then knocked on Joe and Luke's door. They were already up.

"What's happening?" Joe wanted to know. When Nancy told him about her conversation with the captain, he was furious.

"I could kill that guy with my bare hands," Joe seethed. "That's my brother and George who are being held. This guy's job is to find them."

"The question now is, what can *we* do?" Luke said, as Bess came into the room ready for the day in a pair of stretch jeans and a pale peach top. Whenever there was an emergency, Bess could get it together quickly.

"Morita says we can't talk to Heather and Harry," Nancy told her. "We've got to come up with some other way to find George and Frank."

"Let's go over everything we know so far," Joe suggested. "Maybe we're overlooking something."

"Good idea, Joe," Nancy said. "But let's do it over breakfast. I'm starved."

Heading out to a coffee shop across the street, the four went over the case, step by step. Nancy took notes on a pad of hotel paper.

"We know that Heather and Harry are two of the three who were stealing artworks," Joe started.

"I think we can assume that Willy is the third," Nancy said.

"I'd bet on it at this point," Joe said.

"Also, we know they've got to be tied in with the murder of Felix Hoffman, because otherwise, they wouldn't have been searching our Jeep," Nancy continued. "We know someone with a limp broke into our suite. That could be either Johnny Leong or Willy. We also know Harry and Johnny Leong are brothers, and that Johnny was sneaking around the Grand Hawaiian after Rachel told him to stay away," she continued. "Which brings up the matter of your father's packages, Luke."

They all turned to Luke. "We know you're not one of them," Joe said sympathetically. "But is it possible that your father—"

"My father? No way!" Luke said hotly. "My father is a holy man. He's dedicated to saving these islands, not destroying them."

"But how do you know if for money—" Joe didn't get any further.

"You see how my parents live. They're not into money. They're not into glamour. They're into preserving the best of Hawaii, and all of nature, for that matter. There is no way my parents would ever cooperate with people who were stealing Hawaiian treasures."

Nancy and Joe exchanged a glance. "Luke," Nancy said. "It's possible that someone may be duping your father. He may be involved as some kind of innocent accessory."

Luke nodded sadly. "I guess that could be."

"Hoffman, the art thefts, the kidnapping, the stolen money—this whole operation seems incredibly elaborate," Joe said.

"Right," Nancy agreed thoughtfully. "They must have had people tailing us from the time we were in the Grand Hawaiian to when we got off the plane in order to run us down." The face of the driver of the car flashed through her mind again.

"You know, I'm sure I've seen the face of the guy who ran us down somewhere before," Nancy said, playing with her eggs. "Did he look familiar to any of you?"

They all shook their heads, and Nancy sighed. "It must have been when none of you were around—"

"Who could the big man be," Bess wondered. "Big man . . . big man . . ."

"Oh, no. I've got to go call my dad," Nancy said. "I haven't checked in with him since we left Honolulu." She headed back to the pay phone in the rear of the coffee shop.

The hotel operator paged Carson, and after a few minutes, he picked up.

Nancy filled her father in on everything that had happened, up to and including the part about Morita wanting her off the case.

"I know it must be hard for you," Carson said, "but I've got to admit I'd feel better if—"

"How's everything at the Grand Hawaiian?" Nancy asked, abruptly changing the subject.

"Rachel's having stomach problems, bad ones," he said. "I've been trying to talk her into seeing a doctor, but she won't do it. She keeps drinking this strange tea, which smells awful. She claims it helps—"

A light bulb flicked on in Nancy's brain. Kame Kilauea had told them about the curative flowers of the mao plant. Could Rachel's tea be made from mao flowers? "Is it made with yellow flowers?" Nancy asked.

"Why, yes," Carson said, surprised. "How did you know?"

"Just a lucky guess," Nancy replied, her mind racing now. "Dad, what's been bothering Rachel? I know her stomach acts up whenever she's under stress."

"Oh, it's this business about her silent partner again," Carson said disgustedly. "If only I could talk to her and her partner together, we could map out a strategy to defend her hotel from an unfriendly takeover. But apparently, there's no way. The big man doesn't want his identity revealed, so—"

"What?" Nancy gasped. "Did you say, the 'big man'?"

"Yes, that's what she calls him," Carson Drew said. "But, listen, Nan. I'm a lot more worried about your safety right now."

Nancy assured her father that they were all okay and that they'd be back in Honolulu soon. After hanging up, she went back to the table, her head spinning.

"Big man . . . big man . . ." she repeated to herself as she walked. Big in the sense of big boss. A person with enough money to buy a large share of the Grand Hawaiian Hotel, enough criminal contacts to head a gang of art thieves, enough power to keep a gang of several crooks at his disposal, and the organizational ability to plan a whole crime wave.

She sat back down, deep in thought. "This is even bigger than we imagined," she said to the rest of them. "Much bigger—"

There was that word again. *Big.* All at once the pockmarked face of the driver floated to the front of her brain again. Behind the wheel of a car, but not the car that had run them off the road. Another car—a bigger car . . .

Nancy leapt up from her chair. "I've got to go back across the street for a minute!" she cried, running out before anyone could question her. Nancy flew back up to her and Bess's room, ran to the bed, and dumped the contents of her handbag onto the bedspread.

There it was! Good. She hadn't thrown it out. The face on the magazine cover she'd gotten the other day peered straight into the camera, as if he were looking right into Nancy's eyes. The big, pockmarked face of the driver.

The big man was not driving, though. He was sitting in the backseat, his arms raised in front of his face, blocking it from view.

"You can hide from the cameras, Mr. Big Man," Nancy said, grinning. "But you can't hide from me!"

Chapter

Twenty

R AMI TANGA." Back in the coffee shop, Nancy said the name to her friends as if she were announcing the winner of an Academy Award. "He's the big man, I'm positive of it." She handed Joe the magazine cover. "Is that or is that not the guy who ran us down on the road to Hana?" she asked.

"That's him, all right!" Joe exclaimed.

"He's Tanga's personal chauffeur," Nancy pointed out, showing them the identifying caption. "That's Tanga in the backseat, ducking from the cameras. There's a better picture of him inside." She flipped the pages to the photograph.

The photo was of a small man with slicked-back black hair shaking the hand of the United

States ambassador. Obviously, it had been taken when Tanga was still in control of the Torquesas. Joe read the entire article aloud to the others. For him and Bess, most of it was new information.

" ' "The environment of the Torquesa Islands may never fully recover," said the country's new prime minister, Mildred Manto. "Tanga allowed polluting industries free access to our small country, even allowing the outer islands to be used as nuclear test sites. The profits from these damaging activities were all diverted to Tanga's huge personal fortune." ' Wow," Joe said, with disgust. "This guy is a real expert at looking out for number one."

Bess leaned over and continued reading. " 'Tanga is currently residing in Hawaii, where he was given asylum by the U.S. government. The new democratically elected government now seeks the billions he is said to have looted from the treasury. The former strongman has three estates in Hawaii—one on Oahu, one on Maui, and one on the island of Hawaii, also known as the Big Island.' "

"Hey!" Luke exclaimed. "Palaces one, two, and three—from the petroglyph code!"

"Of course!" Nancy said, snapping her fingers. "That's it. George and Frank could even be here at the one on Maui. But then again, maybe not."

Joe slammed his fist down on the table. "Okay," he said, his blue eyes shining. "All we have to do now is find out where Tanga's houses are and go after them one by one."

"Not so fast, Joe," Nancy cautioned. "I think we'd better contact the police. They're much better equipped to negotiate George and Frank's release."

"Negotiate?" Joe asked. "We can't negotiate with those animals!"

"Joe," Luke said, "calm down, man. You can't go busting in on someone like Tanga. He'll be surrounded by armed guards."

"Okay, okay, I admit I'm getting carried away," Joe said. "It's just that I really want to cream this guy."

"The police can do it better," Nancy said.

"They've got the weapons, Joe," Bess pointed out. "We don't."

"So why are we sitting here, then?" Joe said impatiently. "Let's go see Morita."

They paid their bill and drove off in their latest rented car, a silver Subaru.

"Remember to take it easy, Joe," Nancy said as they traveled. "Morita wants us off this case. We've got to be careful how we approach him."

It seemed like forever before they finally convinced the officer at the front desk to call Captain Morita out of his interrogation session. The captain greeted them in a very bad mood. "I thought I told you to stay out of this," he told them, loosening his tie and rubbing what looked like a day-old beard.

"Captain," Nancy said, jumping in with both feet. "I knew you'd want to hear some new information we've gotten. We think it might help—"

"We know who's behind everything—the art thefts, the kidnapping, the murder," Joe broke in. "Everything!"

Nancy shot Joe a cautionary look, but he was too caught up in what he was saying to notice. "It's Rami Tanga," Joe said triumphantly.

"George and Frank must be at one of his estates," Bess added hopefully.

Morita's eyes widened in amazement. "Are you kids out of your minds?" he said slowly. "Rami Tanga? Do you realize what you're saying?"

"Captain," Nancy broke in. "We've identified the man who tried to run us down. He's Rami Tanga's personal chauffeur. Here's his picture." She showed him the magazine photo.

The captain slowly raised his eyes from the photo to Nancy. "You're absolutely certain this was the man?" he asked her.

"Positive," Nancy assured him.

"I saw him, too," Joe put in.

For once Morita seemed to take what they were saying seriously. He sat down on a bench for a few moments, thinking. "Look," he said finally, "if I go after even one of Tanga's staff, let alone the man himself, it starts a whole international incident, you understand? I'll take in the chauffeur, if you insist it was him. But even if he did try to run you down, how does that implicate

Tanga? For that matter, how do I know the chauffeur tried to run you down at all? For all I know, the whole thing was an accident and you kids overreacted."

"Why you—" Joe seemed ready to bust Morita in the mouth, until Nancy put a restraining hand on his arm.

"Captain, please, listen," she began, then outlined their suspicions of Tanga in detail, from his connection to the art thefts to the murder of Felix Hoffman.

Even after hearing all that, Morita seemed unimpressed. "Where's the evidence?" he said with a maddening shrug. "I can't get a search warrant because you think he's got your friends. This is a delicate diplomatic matter—Rami Tanga is an international figure, a VIP. You need proof."

"You mean you're not going to do *anything* about it?" Bess asked, sounding dismayed.

"I didn't say that," the captain said more gently. "I promise we'll keep an eye on Tanga and if we get any indication your friends are being held by him, we'll—we'll certainly take appropriate measures."

Nancy sighed and stared at the floor. It seemed that Joe was right this time—they should have gone in on their own.

"What's more," the captain went on, "you're all to go back to Oahu at once. I'll have my people escort you by helicopter." Before they could protest, he summoned Rivera and Jones, the two officers the teens had met before. "Take these kids back to the Grand Hawaiian, will you?"

As they walked out to the helicopter their mood was anything but cheerful. "Joe," Nancy said quietly, "you were right. We should have gone ahead without telling the police."

Joe shook his head and sighed. "No, you were right, Nan," he said. "We couldn't have out-gunned Tanga and his gang by ourselves."

Luke, who had been fairly quiet most of the day, took Nancy's hand in one of his, and Joe's hand in the other. He beckoned Bess to take Joe and Nancy's hands, too, so they formed a circle. "My people say that where there's unity, evil will not survive," he said, squeezing their hands gently.

Nancy smiled at Luke, who grinned back. He did have a way of making her feel better.

"Okay, kids, here we go," Officer Jones said, interrupting the moment. "Hop on board." Within minutes, they were airborne and on their way to Oahu.

When Rivera and Jones delivered them to Nancy's suite in the Grand Hawaiian, Rivera issued a strong warning. "Stay put. You hear?"

Jones wagged a slender brown finger at them. "We're putting you on the honor system. Don't mess up, or you'll be in trouble."

It seemed the officers had other matters to attend to, which was fine with Nancy.

As soon as the police were out of sight, she

gathered her friends around her. "Here's what we do," she said. "Bess, you and Joe go rent a Jeep. Luke, use the lobby phone to call your father to see if he knows anyone from the Swiss institute who's here in Hawaii. I'll find out where Tanga's Oahu estate is. Then we can ride over and do some snooping."

"Now you're talking," Joe said happily. "Come on, Bess."

After her friends were gone, Nancy dialed the number on the card Ana Saleo had given her. Ms. Saleo told her to come to her hotel, which was one of the high rises.

When Nancy told her of her suspicions of Rami Tanga, Ms. Saleo was aghast, but not surprised.

"It all makes perfect sense," she said softly. "Tanga always had powerful ties with the underworld. International syndicates did a lot of their money-laundering in the Torquesas. They and Tanga were great friends. So if you tell me Tanga is stealing art treasures, I can tell you that he'd know how to sell those treasures to private collectors—through his underworld friends.

"As for the murder of the poor man in the parking lot, you say he worked for a Swiss bank. Tanga has a lot of money in numbered Swiss accounts. Remember I told you he has many couriers to bring the money in and out?"

"Yes, I remember," Nancy said. "You think that Hoffman was one of those couriers?"

"He may have been," Ms. Saleo guessed.

"And if he had stolen some of the money for himself, Tanga might have killed him for it," Nancy said, finishing the thought. "It makes perfect sense! Then, when they couldn't find the money, Tanga must have thought George and I had it. That's why our room and our Jeep were ransacked. That's why they kidnapped George and Frank!"

Ms. Saleo smiled and put a hand on Nancy's shoulder. "You are a very courageous young woman," she told Nancy. "I wish you safety and luck in rescuing your friends. If you can prove Tanga is guilty, you will strike a great victory for the people of the Torquesas."

"That's very comforting," Nancy said with a sigh. "But first we need the proof—and we need to find Frank and George. I came here because I hoped you could tell me how to find Tanga's estates. The newspapers don't disclose the locations, and they aren't listed anywhere—"

"I'll give you a map," Ms. Saleo said. "But don't let anyone know I gave it to you. Tanga has some very important supporters here in the U.S."

"I'll be discreet," Nancy promised. Map in hand, she returned to the Grand Hawaiian to try to find her father.

Carson Drew was more than a little surprised to see his daughter standing next to his table in the café during the ABA lunch break. She joined him for lunch and explained everything.

"Dad, I know how this is going to sound to

you," Nancy said, leaning toward him with her hands folded on the table, "but I believe that Rachel's silent partner may be Rami Tanga."

"Rami Tanga? I'd be hard-pressed to think of Rachel tied up with a character like Tanga."

"But, Dad, it's logical," Nancy explained, wishing that what she was about to say wouldn't hurt him. "Rachel needed cash, and she got some when she took on her silent partner. Suppose it was Tanga? Wouldn't the Grand Hawaiian be the perfect place for his couriers to meet him?"

Carson had put his fork down to listen intently.

"Kame Kilauea could have given them cover without knowing it by providing packages to hide the flow of money, packages with scientific labels—the kind customs would lay off. Maybe Rachel gave him the use of the hotel as a way to keep the Grand Hawaiian alive."

"I have to admit, your theory would explain a great deal of Rachel's behavior. But she'd never knowingly be a part of the art thefts, not to mention kidnapping and murder."

Nancy wasn't sure anymore, but she kept her suspicions to herself. "I think we should go see her, don't you?" she suggested.

Carson got up. "Lead the way," he said, signing his card and getting up from the table.

Soon they arrived at Rachel's office. Her secretary was just coming out, her arms full of papers. "Ms. Maxon's not in," she was quick to say. Nancy noticed that the secretary positioned herself between them and Rachel's office door. "She's gone for the weekend."

"That's strange," Carson said. "I just saw her an hour ago. She didn't say anything."

As the secretary was about to respond, Nancy took advantage of the moment to brush past her into Rachel's office. "I'll only be a second," Nancy said breezily, stepping inside.

"Oh, no, you can't go in th—" the secretary said too late. Nancy was staring in disbelief at the office, which had obviously been emptied in a great hurry. Rachel's desktop was totally clear as were the shelves adjacent to her desk.

"What the—?" Carson started to say.

"Please leave!" the secretary insisted.

"We're leaving," Nancy shot back, stalling for time. Then she saw something intriguing sticking out of the wastebasket.

It was a large envelope—with Kame Kilauea's label on it!

Retrieving it from the trash, Nancy quickly left the room. "I was looking for an envelope just this size," she said, "and since it was in the trash, I'll just take it. 'Bye." With that, Nancy walked from the room.

Glancing down, she could hardly believe her good luck. She was holding something vitally important to figuring out the case. That envelope was what she'd been searching for. It was her first piece of concrete evidence—evidence that linked Rachel Maxon to the murder in the parking garage—and to Rami Tanga.

Chapter
Twenty-One

"Let's go, Dad." Nancy put her arm through her father's and started quickly walking away from Rachel's office. Her excitement at finding a major clue was lessened because of her father's disappointment. Still, if Rachel Maxon was involved in this business, he'd have to find out about it sooner or later.

As they walked, Nancy held up the envelope. "Customs opens most business briefcases. But I bet they go easy on couriers carrying scientific ones, as long as the organizations sending them are established and ethical. The first several packages sent to Switzerland—which customs would have opened—more than likely had nothing but healing plants in them," she said. "That would have built up customs' trust. Only later would Tanga's agents have put money inside. That's the way I see it, anyway."

"I find it hard to believe that Rachel would participate in something like this, Nancy," her father said. "Isn't it possible that she didn't know about or understand this scheme? Tanga might have duped her into it."

"Like he duped Big Man Kame?" Nancy said. "Could be, Dad."

Carson seemed to be quite shaken and no wonder. It seemed that Rachel had, at best, poor judgment—and at worst, bad character.

"Gee, Dad," Nancy said, reaching over and giving him a hug. There wasn't much she could say right then to make him feel better, but she had to let him know she cared.

"I guess Rachel ran away because she knew you were getting close to the truth," he said bravely.

Nancy nodded sympathetically as she pushed open the door of the stairwell. "Right now I'd trade everything I know about Rachel if I could just find out where George and Frank are, and how to get them out. I can't let them down!"

"How can I help?" Carson asked, following Nancy up the stairs to the fourth floor.

"You can try to find Rachel for me and keep an eye on her," Nancy told him, stopping on a landing. "Dad," she began, "we have a plan." She told him exactly how she and her friends intended to find George and Frank.

Listening, Carson didn't look happy. "Nancy,

181

that's much too dangerous," he said firmly. "This is a job for the police!"

"The police have practically told us they're not going to get involved with anything that has to do with Tanga," Nancy explained.

"But Tanga's men will be armed," Carson said.

"I know," Nancy said. "But don't worry—"

"Don't worry? Last time you told me that you were nearly killed!" he exclaimed.

"I promise, Dad, we'll be super careful," Nancy said. "Tanga's men aren't even going to know we're there. As soon as we spot any sign of George or Frank, we'll contact the police. *They'll* be the ones to go in for them."

"And you're going to do this today?" he asked.

"If we're not back in three hours, call the cops," Nancy told him. "We've decided to check out Tanga's Oahu estate as long as we're here. The last we heard, Frank and George were probably on Maui, but it's logical they'd be moved around."

"All right," Carson said, giving in. "But please, Nan—be careful. I don't want to lose you."

"You won't," she assured him.

Climbing the last stairs, they turned into the corridor toward Nancy's suite. At the door, Carson gave her one last hug. She hugged him back, hard.

"Good luck," Carson said, when they broke apart. "I'm going to try to find Rachel. Maybe she can clear up some of this nasty business."

Luke told Nancy, Joe, and Bess about his

phone call to his father. "My father said the Swiss institute has always been very secretive about their organization. They never gave him the names of any of their people in Hawaii. Still, Dad felt he had no reason not to trust them. When I told him what we'd uncovered, he was sick," Luke said. "He's going to start a campaign to petition the governor to bring Rami Tanga to justice."

"Good luck to him," Nancy said. "Somehow, I don't think it's up to the governor, in this case."

"Well, who's it up to, then?" Luke asked.

Nancy dropped into a chair and turned to her friends. "Guys," she said, "it's up to *us.*"

"Frank Hardy?" Captain Morita's voice conveyed astonishment over the phone line. "This is *Frank Hardy?"*

"Yes, Captain," Frank said. "It's me all right." It had taken nearly twenty minutes to track down the captain, who was in Maui, much to Frank's surprise.

"Are you okay?" Morita asked. "They haven't hurt you?"

"They tried," Frank said.

"Where's the girl? Is she with you?" Morita wanted to know.

"Not now," Frank told him.

"Where are you now?" the captain asked.

"I have no idea," Frank said. "I'm on the Big Island, I know that much, on a back road somewhere, at a public phone booth. I'm in the middle of nowhere. There are no houses, nothing."

"Hang on, I'll have the call traced and then have someone pick you up. Stay put," said the captain. There was a click, and then nothing. Frank held on, staring out at the bright morning sky. That strange orange glow still lit up the horizon.

By two that afternoon, Nancy and the others had arrived at Rami Tanga's Oahu estate. They parked the car on the side of the road about a quarter mile from the mansion.

When they got close enough to see it, Luke put up his hand. "Let me teach you how my people walk silently through the jungle," he said. "Step toe first, on the edge of your foot. It will help all of us now."

Nancy did what he described, and smiled. "This will be a very useful skill," she said, impressed. They edged up to the estate.

The huge sprawling grounds were surrounded by a tall iron gate and lush flowering bougainvillea.

Bess peered through an opening in the bushes and said, "Looks like Tanga spent a fortune on this place."

Nancy nodded. The ornate mansion was the one she had seen in the newspaper photo.

"Check out those statues," Joe said, pointing to marble nymphs guarding the mansion's front entrance. "This guy has no taste at all."

"Careful," Nancy cautioned, "we're getting close to the main gate."

Hiding behind the bushes, the teens saw a security booth next to the huge ornate iron entrance gate of the estate. The booth was manned by a poker-faced guard in a fancy uniform, who sat working a crossword puzzle in a book. At his feet slept a large Doberman.

"The house is a good two hundred yards away," Joe whispered. "How will we be able to see anything from here?"

Luke reached over and tapped Nancy on the shoulder. He signaled them to go back the way they'd come, a place beside the fence where the land rose. That's got to be the best place to observe from, Nancy thought. They silently started up the rise.

From the top they had a clear view of the mansion in the distance. Nancy saw a four-car garage in back, all four doors open. "Look for Frank's car," Bess urged breathlessly in Nancy's ear.

"There's a Lincoln Continental," Nancy murmured, her binoculars to her eyes, "and a Rolls-Royce. That's all."

"What about the windows? Can you see in any of them?" Joe asked.

Nancy focused her binoculars on several of the windows of the house, one at a time. "I can't tell a thing," Nancy said quietly. "I don't see anyone stirring. It may not mean anything, but I have a feeling Frank and George aren't here." The others agreed.

Luke whispered, "Let's get away from here. We can talk someplace else."

Nancy put her binoculars up for one last look. "You guys," she whispered. "I see something."

She quickly handed the binoculars to Joe so he could look, too. "He's got an overnight bag with him, and he's holding an airline ticket. He's getting in the Lincoln," Joe whispered.

"Who? Who?" Bess wanted to know.

Nancy was the first to answer. "It's someone we know, Bess—Willy Brannigan!"

"He must be headed for the airport. Come on!" Joe cried, sprinting back toward the car.

Joe got into the driver's seat, slammed the door, and gunned the engine as they all piled in. As soon as the last door was shut, he took off for the airport.

"What if Willy isn't going to the airport, Joe?" Luke asked.

"We still have to go to the airport. We've got to check Tanga's other estates, remember? The one on Maui, and the other one on the Big Island."

"Right," Nancy answered.

"Maui first," Joe said.

"I agree," said Luke for all of them. "That's where the ransom call came from, that's where we were told to bring the money, that's where the big guy tried to run us off the road. . . ."

Half an hour later Nancy was reading the

airport video terminal. She said, "The next flight to the Big Island is in two hours. There's a flight to Maui boarding right now, at Gate Twenty-one."

"Great," Joe said. "Maui it is."

Nancy led the group to the nearest counter. "Four to Maui, please," she told the attendant.

Just then Luke pointed outside to the runways. "What's going on out there?"

They saw a flurry of police cars drawing up to a police plane. "What do you suppose—?" Bess began.

Joe was quicker than any of them. "I'll go check it out. I'll meet you at Gate Twenty-one. Don't let the plane take off without me," he called over his shoulder as he raced past a security guard.

"Hey, you!" shouted the startled guard. "Where's your boarding pass?" Joe was already out on the runway with two guards chasing him.

Nancy and the others stood watching the drama unfold. By the time the guards caught up with Joe, he had already talked to a mechanic.

"We have to get on board," Nancy said, turning away from the window. "Hurry!" She and Bess and Luke ran to Gate Twenty-one and stepped onto their plane.

"What about Joe?" Bess asked, distressed.

"We'll just have to think of a way to—" Nancy began, but she was soon interrupted by a frantic flight attendant.

"Sir, I told you I can't let you on without a ticket," the flight attendant was insisting.

"I don't want to go on," Joe's voice came back. "Nancy! Bess! Luke!" he shouted. "Get off the plane, quick! You're on your way to the wrong island!"

Chapter

Twenty-Two

THE WRONG ISLAND?" Nancy repeated, embarrassed by the commotion she and her friends were making. "Excuse me, please," she said, passing a man who was loading his bag into an overhead compartment.

"Come on, Luke," Bess said, following Nancy off the plane.

Joe was waiting for them with a security guard at his elbow.

"What's going on, Joe?" Nancy pressed, the moment the guard left them alone and was out of earshot.

"Rivera and Jones are on their way to the Big Island," Joe said, as they made their way back to the ticket counters. "I heard Morita's already left

189

for there from the mechanic I spoke to. That must be where the action is."

"Maybe they've found George and Frank!" Bess said enthusiastically.

Bess was assuming that if George and Frank were found, they'd be alive. Nancy wasn't so sure.

"Good work, Joe," Nancy told him, shaking that last thought off with a shudder. "Let's go exchange our tickets. I just wish we didn't have a two-hour wait."

"What if we hire an air taxi to take us there?" Luke suggested. "There should be one around here somewhere."

"Good idea," Nancy said. While Luke went to hire an air taxi, Nancy put in a call to her father, but he wasn't in his suite. She left a message saying everything was fine, and that she'd check back in another three hours.

Forty minutes later the teens climbed aboard a six-seater and took off into the glorious Hawaiian sunset.

"Let's figure out a course of action," Nancy said, forcing her attention away from the spectacular reds and golds showing in the sky. "I have a map that Ana Saleo made for us right here in my purse."

"And here's a tourist map of the Big Island," Joe said, pulling a folded paper from his back pocket.

"According to Ana's map," Nancy said,

"Tanga's home is here, near Volcano National Park."

"The goddess calls for her revenge," Luke said, his face serious as he gazed out into the clouds.

"What are you saying?" Nancy asked respectfully.

"Tanga built his estate near the home of Pele," Luke said, his dark eyes shining. "Now Pele will find him."

When the plane landed, Nancy sent Bess to find the nearest Rent-A-Wreck car agency. "It's the best idea," Nancy said. "We've been kind of hard on cars lately."

Within half an hour they'd eaten some sandwiches and climbed into a 1974 Plymouth Scamp.

"Don't put your foot down too hard," Bess warned Joe from the backseat. "The man said it's rusty under there."

"You really think this car can make it up the slope of Kilauea?" Luke asked doubtfully.

Nancy turned back and gave him a grin. "This car has a slant six engine," she explained. "It's the best."

It took about half an hour to reach Volcano National Park. "It's hard to see now because it's dark," Luke told them all, "but this area has fields of lava for miles on end. It looks kind of like a moonscape."

"What's that weird orange color in the sky?" Bess asked, peering out the window.

"My namesake, Kilauea," Luke explained. "The flowing lava colors the sky."

"Flowing lava?" Bess repeated. "You mean, like, molten rock? A thousand degrees or so?"

"Kilauea is an active volcano, Bess," Joe said. "It's not extinct like Haleakala."

"Don't worry, Bess," Luke told her. "Kilauea often erupts, but the eruptions are small."

"Small eruptions? That's comforting," Bess said, sounding anything but comforted.

"Joe, take over driving, okay?" Nancy slowed down and pulled off the road. "I have to check Ana's map."

"I need to stretch, anyway," Bess said.

When they got out, she walked a few feet away from the car and suddenly screamed. "There's something down there! I felt a hot breath on my leg!"

"Don't worry, Bess," Luke said, laughing and putting an arm around her shoulder. "You were just standing near a sulfur vent." He released her and knelt down as Nancy shone her penlight on the ground. Hot smoke was rising from a narrow crack in the grass.

"Pee-yew, something stinks," Joe said as the breeze changed directions.

"That smell is sulfur coming from the vent," Luke explained. "The activity of the inner earth is close to the surface here. There are sulfur vents and lava tubes and—"

"Lava tubes?" Joe asked.

"They're tunnels that hot lava has carved

under the earth," Luke told him. "Some go on for miles. In an eruption, they often carry the molten rock long distances."

"Wow," Joe said. "The power of volcanoes is incredible."

"The power of the goddess Pele is incredible," Luke quietly corrected him. For one enchanted moment, the teens stared transfixed at the eerie orange glow in the sky.

"Let's go on," Nancy said, getting back into the car. "We should be there soon."

They climbed higher still, with the land dropping off sharply to the ocean on their left.

"Can you imagine this place by day?" Joe said, staring out into the night. "Pretty wild."

"Tanga sure picks nice locations for his mansions," Bess added dryly.

"Ana Saleo called his Big Island estate the country palace," Nancy said. "Apparently he comes here to get away from all the pressures of being a world-class billionaire and thug."

"There's a pay phone in that gas station," Joe pointed out as they passed through a small mountainside village. "If we need to call the police, we'll come back down here and use it."

"According to this map, Joe," Nancy said, "the dirt road to the estate begins exactly one point five miles past the church we just passed. Let's keep our eyes on the odometer."

After a mile and a half, they saw the merest trace of a dirt road leading into dense jungle. "That's got to be it," Nancy said. "We'll leave the car here. The estate should be a few hundred yards up the road." They all got out, and started hiking through the foliage alongside the dirt road. Nancy reasoned they would be safer off the main entrance drive.

She could almost tell what Joe was thinking. What they were doing now was the most dangerous thing they'd done so far—and they'd done some pretty dangerous things.

"Maybe Bess should stay behind," Joe suggested. "That way, if someone comes down the road, she can beep the car horn to warn us."

"No, Joe," Nancy objected. "We've got a good plan, let's go with it. Bess is safer with us. If we see any sign of George or Frank, we'll run back to the car and get the police."

"I guess you're right," Joe said. "Okay, let's go. No more noise."

After a few minutes of stalking through the vegetation, they saw a wrought-iron gate with ornate spikes on top. Beyond the gate was a sweeping lawn, and in the distance the mansion, a long, low, hacienda-style ranch, was visible. Light from inside the house fell onto the lawn in long rectangles.

"He's probably got motion-sensitive security," Nancy whispered, using the stalking step Luke had taught them to approach the fence. "If we get too close, we may be doused with floodlights."

"So what do we do?" Joe murmured.

"Well, I know what I'm going to do," Luke

announced in a whisper. "You all stay here. I'm going to walk right up to the gate and announce myself. Then I'm going in the front door to see who's in there."

"What?" Joe said incredulously. "You're out of your mind! They'll kidnap you, too. Not only that, they'll know the rest of us are here!"

"Not if I tell them I got a flat tire down the road and ask to use their phone," Luke insisted. "Look, they don't know me. The only one who saw me for sure is Heather, and she's in jail."

Joe opened his mouth to protest, but Luke cut him off.

"We've got to find out if Frank and George are here," Luke continued. "If I get in and don't come out in half an hour, it'll mean I'm being held. That's reason enough to call the police."

"It's risky, but I'll go for it," Nancy said.

Bess was incredulous. "Luke, aren't you afraid? They might kill you!"

"Here, in the home of Pele, I cannot be afraid," he answered.

In the face of that kind of courage, Nancy, Joe, and Bess could only watch the young Hawaiian as he walked to the gate. Soon bright lights flooded the lawn, and Luke's lonely figure strode to the front door and disappeared inside.

"He's brave, I'll say that for him," Joe said admiringly.

"Good-looking, too," Bess added with a sigh.

* * *

The next half hour was endless. "Should we give him another five minutes?" Bess wondered when his time was up.

"He said half an hour," Joe said. "It's up. Bess, go to the car. Drive on back to the gas station and call the police."

"Here are the keys," Nancy told her. "Don't press the accelerator too many times, or the engine will flood."

"How many times is too many?" Bess asked, her hands on her hips.

"I don't know," Nancy said. "It's a touch thing. You have to feel it."

"I don't know about this," Bess murmured as she hurried back toward the main road.

"Run, Bess," Nancy called softly after her.

When she was gone, Nancy and Joe gave each other a look. "What now?" she asked him.

"I'd say the only thing to do is to go in," Joe said. He was trying to sound matter-of-fact, but Nancy could hear the edge in his voice.

"Okay," Nancy agreed.

Without talking, they walked to the front gate.

"We're in luck," Joe whispered. "There's no guard here, and Luke left the gate open." Being super quiet, Nancy and Joe slipped through the open gate. Then, under the starlit sky, they made their way closer to the house, using bushes and trees for cover. "No dogs, no loud alarms, no security guards," Joe said confusedly. "I don't get it."

"I don't *like* it, either," Nancy said. The two teens were about fifty feet from the house now. Around the side entrance, a door was open, revealing what looked to be a large sitting room.

"Well, if that's not an invitation, I don't know what is," Joe whispered excitedly. "We're in luck again."

Nancy shivered in the cool night air. "I don't know," she said. "It all seems *too* lucky to me. But it's too late to turn back now."

Nancy heard voices coming from somewhere above them as she and Joe slipped in through the open door. The voices were loud, raised in argument, the voices of a man and a woman. They were too distant and muffled for Nancy to make out their words.

"Let's try down here," Joe whispered, motioning for Nancy to follow him into the hallway.

There were several doors along the hallway. Nancy gently grasped the handles and turned them, but each was locked. Then to her surprise, one opened.

Stepping in, Nancy and Joe found themselves in a room lined with bookshelves on all four walls—a library. The moon cast enough light for Nancy to see the outlines of certain shelves with native Hawaiian artifacts set on them.

"Nancy, look," Joe whispered hoarsely. "Some of the stolen treasures!"

Nancy recognized an onyx mask that gleamed in the moonlight. The face seemed to be warning her to turn back. Nancy blew out a breath and willed her heart to stop racing. If ever she needed a clear head it was now.

"Nan, the Indonesian crown," Joe whispered, holding up a work of gold filigree. "Mr. Watanabe showed us a picture of it."

Scanning the room, Nancy noticed a large wooden totem. As she stepped over to examine it, she tripped and tumbled onto something soft on the floor.

"It's a body—it's Luke!" she gasped in terror.

Joe raced over to see. "He's breathing fine," Joe remarked, kneeling down to check. "There's a gash on his head, but it doesn't look bad."

"Joe," Nancy said, putting a hand on his arm. "The door. The open door. If Luke was knocked out, why did they leave the door open?"

"A very good question," a familiar female voice rang out from the doorway. Nancy gasped as the woman stepped into view.

Rachel Maxon!

Rachel had an automatic pistol in her hand, and it was trained on them. "I'm so sorry it's come to this, Nancy," Rachel said, a pitying look in her eyes. "You should have left Hawaii when you had the chance."

Chapter
Twenty-Three

Rachel Maxon advanced into the room, followed by an old man Nancy had never seen before. He had a long, sparse white beard.

"Go get the big man," Rachel told him.

"Are you sure you can manage these two?" the old man asked her.

"Of course I'm sure," Rachel said, irritation creeping into her voice.

"I'll send our boys to help you," the old man said. His steely-eyed gaze had sized Rachel up and found her wanting. Then he glided out the room, leaving Rachel alone with Nancy and Joe.

"Don't get any bright ideas," Rachel warned, raising the gun. "I'm an expert shot, and I won't hesitate to kill you if I have to."

"You're going to kill us, anyway, aren't you?" Joe asked.

Rachel's face tightened, and Nancy tried a more conciliatory tack. "Joe, this is Rachel Maxon, who owns the Grand Hawaiian Hotel. She's a friend of my father."

"Some friend," Joe huffed, leaning over Luke, who was still out cold.

"Stand straight," Rachel commanded Joe. Then she turned to Nancy, her voice softening. "Look, I never wanted this to happen."

"Then stop now," Nancy urged her. "Don't make it worse for yourself. My dad can be a very forgiving man—especially when he cares about someone."

Rachel stood silently, the gun still leveled at them. But from the pained expression in Rachel's eyes, Nancy knew she was considering what Nancy said.

"Besides, you haven't really done anything so terrible—yet. Maybe you didn't know that Tanga was using your hotel for criminal activities," Nancy suggested. "Maybe you didn't know about the ring of art thieves Tanga's been running. You can still save yourself, Rachel, and your hotel!"

Rachel backed up a bit, and Nancy saw a tremor shake her body. Nancy could feel Joe on her left, tensed and ready to spring at the first opportunity.

"Rachel," Nancy said, choosing her words carefully, "Rami Tanga ruined the Torquesa Islands. He trashed the environment, cut down the forests, and polluted the water. The Torquesas may never recover. *And now he's here in Hawaii.* What's going to happen if he makes himself a powerful force here? If you love Hawaii, this is the time to prove it!"

Rachel's gun hand started to lower. Squeezing her eyes shut, she clutched at her stomach. Now the gun was dangling from her hands, and Joe started to make his move.

He was stopped short as the huge frame of Tanga's chauffeur filled the doorway, a semiautomatic rifle in his fat hands. Another thug filed in behind. Then one more man entered—a man who moved with a catlike grace that Nancy recognized along with his shiny tan shoes—the killer in the parking garage!

Behind them came the old man with the beard. These people closely spaced themselves around Nancy and Joe as the "Big Man" entered.

Rami Tanga looked even smaller than he had in the newspaper photo. He wore a stylish white linen suit and peach silk shirt open at the collar. On his wrist was an expensive-looking watch. "Welcome to my estate," he said, with a grin that was more of a grimace. "You know, I feel as if I already know you."

"Where are Frank and George?" Joe demanded. "We want to see them!"

"I'm sure you do," Tanga said, amused.

"Why, you—" Despite the danger, Joe lunged at Tanga. The burly chauffeur shoved him back.

Nancy desperately thought of Bess. Had she

made it to a phone and notified the police? Would they be there soon?

"What do you want us to do with them?" the old man asked Tanga.

"Well, since they've come so far to experience these lovely islands," the dictator replied, "I think we should do something special." He turned and smiled at Nancy and Joe. "As your host, I'm going to arrange for you to experience an authentic custom of old Hawaii. I am going to honor you by sacrificing you to Pele." Tanga tried to stifle a cackling laugh, but he didn't succeed. Behind him, his men laughed in a hideous chorus. But not Rachel. She was still staring at Nancy intently.

"You won't get away with it, Tanga!" Joe said. "The police will be here any minute!"

With an amused smile, Tanga snapped his fingers. "I think not, Mr. Wipeout. I think not."

A moment later Willy Brannigan entered, holding Bess in a half-nelson.

"Bess!" Nancy cried.

Willy threw Bess onto the floor at Nancy's feet. Bess struggled to stand with Nancy's help. "Are you all right, Bess?" Nancy asked.

Bess burst into tears. "I couldn't get the car started, Nan. He must have heard me trying. He dragged me all the way here——" Bess massaged her bruised arm as tears streamed down her face.

Nancy turned back to Tanga. "I see that you have all of us now. Since you are going to kill us, may I ask a few questions first?" She was desperate to stall for time and felt sure that Tanga had an ego big enough to want to gloat over his crimes.

"Ask your questions," he said pleasantly. "We have time."

Soon they'd heard the whole story of how Tanga had created a courier system. "I set up the network before I left the Torquesas," he explained proudly. "And when I needed a hotel large enough for my operation, I approached this lovely lady here. She generously allowed me the use of her hotel for my couriers, no questions asked. In exchange I rescued her business. Today I called in my remaining favor, as we agreed."

Nancy watched Rachel. Clearly, she was uncomfortable with her role as a big-time lawbreaker. If only Nancy could get a chance to work on her some more!

"What about Felix Hoffman?" Nancy asked Tanga. "How did he fit in?"

"Felix Hoffman was dipping into my funds," Tanga said bitterly. "I don't like thieves."

Not when they steal from *you*, Nancy thought angrily, but when she spoke, her voice was composed and calm.

"You had people watching us the whole time we were in the hotel, didn't you?" Nancy pressed him.

"But of course." Tanga cracked an evil smile.

"And you had Willy break into our room!" Bess cried.

"Incorrect. It was Johnny Leong, whose leg

your sleeping friend here"—Tanga gestured to Luke—"almost ripped off. Johnny worked for me in the Torquesas," Tanga said, his eyes hardening into little black dots. "It was his idea that I come to Hawaii. The climates are very similar, you know.

"Johnny's brother Harry proved to be a valuable asset, too. Harry is a lover of Hawaiian artifacts, and it was he who advised me on which museums to hit. He also developed the code we sent our instructions in."

"What about Heather and Willy?" Nancy asked, hoping that the police would arrive.

"Curious, aren't you?" Tanga said. "Well, it's no matter, for you will soon be swallowed up by Pele." The dictator smiled slyly and continued, "Heather and Willy are like many of your generation. They are greedy. When they heard that they could make easy money, they readily agreed to work for me."

"Where does Kame Kilauea fit into all this?" she asked.

"Big Man Kame, ah, yes," Tanga said with a chuckle. "I'm afraid the big man was far too anxious to save his medicinal plants to seriously investigate the Swiss institute that contacted him. Kame was very easily duped." Tanga shook his head in mock regret. "By the way, the mao flower does seem to have real value in the pharmaceutical world. I've made a tidy profit dealing with firms in Japan and Korea. And, of course, Rachel has been fortunate to have a steady supply, thanks to me. I'm sure she's very grateful. Aren't you, dear?" Rachel avoided his eyes.

"Where's my brother, Mr. Nice Guy? You didn't answer me the first time I asked," Joe snarled. "Where is he?"

Tanga frowned suddenly. "Your brother Frank just couldn't leave well enough alone. We drugged him at Harry's nightclub, but he just couldn't seem to take a warning. Then he misbehaved at my estate. Our only recourse was to take Frank on a tour of the Big Island, but unfortunately, he had a boating accident on the river. I'm afraid he drowned."

Joe's face went white as Nancy's eyes filled with tears. Bess began to sob.

"Come," Tanga said curtly. "We're wasting time." He snapped his fingers, and two of the men with guns forced the teens out the door. "Put them in the van," Tanga ordered. "We'll follow in the car."

"What about this one?" asked the old man, pointing to Luke, still unconscious on the floor.

"Stay with him," Tanga told the old man and one thug. "We'll still need to find out what his father knows."

"What if he wakes up?" the man in the T-shirt and jeans asked.

"Give him an injection now," Tanga said, "just to make sure." With that, he left the room, and everyone followed.

After binding their wrists, the thugs forced Nancy, Joe, and Bess into a van. On the van floor was the outline of someone else, bound and gagged. George! She was alive!

George raised her head, and the desperation in her eyes made Nancy wish to throw her arms around her friend and ease all her suffering.

Nancy looked over at Joe, but his head was down. His eyes were squeezed shut in private pain—the kind of pain that would never go away.

The van traveled over bumpy, unpaved roads for what felt like an hour. Then it screeched to a halt, and the doors were opened. They were all hauled out onto a deserted road with an eerie orange glow all around. A low sizzling sound hissed in the predawn air.

As the two men pointed guns at them, Tanga, Rachel, and Willy pulled up behind the van and got out of their car. "I thought you'd be interested to see an authentic Hawaiian volcano close up," Tanga said sadistically. "Across the road, blocking our progress, you'll see hardened lava from a previous eruption. It's turned to rock now, but it was once liquid fire. In its molten form, it can vaporize a person in seconds. Come, have a closer look," he added with a chuckle. "Oh, and step carefully. The ground is brittle, and there are many lava tubes beneath the surface. They may even have molten lava running in them. We don't want you to hurt yourselves—yet."

Following Tanga, they crossed the patch of cooled lava and continued on down the road. At a bend they saw a thick stream of red-hot lava flowing down the mountainside above them. Horrified, Nancy realized what Tanga had in store for them!

"There will be no evidence," Tanga said with a smile, signaling to his henchmen. "No bodies will be found. You will simply disappear off the face of the earth."

Chapter

Twenty-Four

THIS ONE FIRST," Tanga ordered his men, pointing to George. Rico and Jonathan bent down and picked George up by her shoulders and feet. She valiantly tried to put up a struggle, but she was bound too tightly. The thugs began trudging with her to where the hot lava sizzled down the slope of the mountain.

Nancy felt Joe's eyes searing into her. Even though their hands were bound, she knew he was signaling her to strike. Nancy nodded, then bent her knees slightly. In an instant she sprang at Tanga, knocking him over before he could react. Bess, too, dove on top of Tanga, helping Nancy to hold him pinned to the ground. Simultaneously, Joe leapt at Willy, ramming his bound fists into

Willy's stomach. Willy doubled over, and Joe threw all his weight on him, tackling him to the ground.

Nancy felt Tanga's fingers digging sharply into her arms as she and Bess struggled to keep the wily dictator down. He was shouting for Rachel to fire her gun, but there was no response.

Out of the corner of her eye, Nancy saw the other two thugs place George about thirty feet from the hot, flowing lava. The hiss and sizzle of the molten rock must have kept them from hearing the struggle, because they paid no attention to Tanga's shouts.

"Rachel!" Nancy shouted hoarsely as Tanga grabbed hold of her. "Don't let them kill us— you'd be a murderer! Rachel!"

Rachel stiffened. Then she turned to Tanga and pointed the gun squarely at him with wild determination in her eyes.

"Untie their hands," Rachel ordered Tanga. He released Nancy first, who ran to help Joe with Willy. At that instant Willy broke away, ran to the van, and gunned the motor. "He's getting away!" Joe yelled, as the van burned rubber and executed a quick U-turn. Before any of them could stop him, Willy was gone.

"Let him go!" Nancy shouted.

Just as Nancy finished Joe's hands, she saw the two thugs trotting back toward them, their automatic pistols drawn.

"Drop the guns!" Rachel shouted, moving behind Tanga and holding her pistol to his head.

The pair slowed to a walk, then stopped just short of Nancy, Bess, and Joe, uncertain what to do.

"Bess, help George!" Nancy shouted, seeing that her friend's hands were no longer bound.

"Nancy, Joe," Rachel called to them. "Take their guns."

As Nancy and Joe reached out, Tanga shrieked, "Get them!" With a quick twist of his body, he turned on Rachel and grabbed her gun hand. At the same time, Nancy and Joe grabbed the weapons.

Her hand around Jonathan's pistol, Nancy struggled to keep the nuzzle away from herself and pointed at him. Beside her, Joe was doing the same. Over Jonathan's shoulder, Nancy saw the hot lava creep closer to George as Bess ran to her rescue.

"Tanga's got Rachel's gun," Joe called out to Nancy, keeping up his struggle with the heavyset chauffeur. Nancy saw Tanga bring the gun down on Rachel's head, knocking her out. Then he straightened up, and raised his gun, aiming straight for Joe!

Nancy's breath caught as the gun fired and a masculine voice uttered a pathetic groan. Don't let it be, she prayed, as she sank her teeth into Jonathan's arm with all the force she could muster.

It was Rico who sank to the ground, wounded. Tanga raised his hand for another shot, just as Jonathan, dropping his gun, screamed in pain.

Grabbing his weapon from the ground, Nancy shouted, "Drop it, Tanga!"

Startled, Tanga's second shot missed its mark. He fired once at Nancy, wildly, then took off running. Joe, freed from the chauffeur's grasp, had tackled Jonathan after Nancy let him go. Joe slammed his fists right on the point of the man's chin, and he went limp.

"Tanga's getting away," Joe cried, watching him scramble over the rocks. "Leave him to me," he shouted, dashing after the dictator.

Nancy ran off to help Bess, who was struggling to drag George out of the path of the lava. George was too heavy for her alone, and Nancy knew there wasn't a second to lose.

Joe ran after Tanga, but all at once Tanga seemed to disappear into the earth.

Then Joe saw it—a small hole in the ground. The entrance to a lava tube. Tanga must be hiding in there! Joe lowered himself into the dark, empty tube. Immediately he heard footsteps echoing off the walls. He took off after Tanga and was gaining as they ran uphill in the semidarkness.

Tanga ducked around a bend, with Joe in hot pursuit.

Then Joe heard a new sound—a sizzling, bubbling sound. All at once, there was a hideous scream from Tanga, and a long hiss. The next thing Joe knew, a stream of orange lava was coming around the bend, headed straight for him! Not stopping to think about Rami Tanga's grisly end, Joe turned and ran for his life. The lava boiled after him, gaining every second. At the last possible instant, Joe found the hole by which he'd come in. He hoisted himself out just as the molten rock streamed past the spot.

Emerging into the gathering light of dawn, Joe ran back to the spot where he and Nancy had first struggled with Tanga and his men. The two thugs were surrounded by a group of police! Rico, who'd been hit, was bleeding from his arm. Rachel still lay on the ground, with Nancy, George, and Bess beside her.

Captain Morita was there. So were Luke—and Frank!

"Frank!" Joe yelled wildly, racing to give his brother a hug. "Boy, am I glad to see you!"

"Same here, little brother," Frank said with a smile. "Are you okay?"

Joe nodded. "I'm all right, but Tanga—a lava flow got him," he said.

"Pele's had her revenge," Luke said solemnly.

Captain Morita came forward to explain. "Frank led us to Tanga's mansion," he said. "When we got there, we caught the old man and Tanga's other thug by surprise. They told us where you were. Right now my men are going through the house, looking for the money."

"What about Willy?" Nancy asked. "He's still out there somewhere."

Morita laughed and shook his head. "Believe it or not, he was picked up for speeding. Oh, and we got Johnny Leong, too—he was the major courier between Tanga and the Grand Hawaiian, it seems. We'll have the whole gang in custody pretty soon."

Rachel was coming back to consciousness now. Nancy bent over her, helping her to a sitting position. "What will happen to Rachel?" she asked Morita. "She tried to help us. We'd be dead if it wasn't for her, Captain."

Morita frowned. "Well, she's in some trouble, that's for sure," he said. "But if what you're saying is true, the court may be lenient."

"You've done a great service for Hawaii," Luke told Nancy and the Hardys.

"You've helped the Torquesas, too," Captain Morita put in. "They'll be able to recover their money, now, thanks to you. I'm afraid I did you many disservices, and I apologize."

"Apology accepted," Nancy said, speaking for all of them. "We're just glad everything worked out all right."

George, Frank, Joe, Bess, and Carson were sitting at an outdoor café on Waikiki Beach. Frank was digging into his third hamburger, and George was on her second plate of food.

"I'm glad I finally got to see who Nancy was spending so much time with," Carson said, grinning at Frank and Joe. "You make quite a team."

"It's your daughter who saved the day," Joe said. "Nancy's the one who figured out that it was Tanga's chauffeur who ran us off the road."

"What's that about me?" Nancy said, walking up and sitting down next to her father. "I just got off the phone with Captain Morita."

"Did he tell you what happened to the money?" Bess asked.

"Give me a chance and I'll tell you," Nancy teased. "First of all, Harry and Heather and Willy confessed to committing the museum robberies. They're hoping to get lighter sentences in exchange for cooperating."

"But did the cops find the money?" George asked, between bites.

"It was hidden under a couch in the sitting room in the Oahu mansion," Nancy said. "And they even found documents proving that Tanga had stolen the Torquesas' money, along with a list of names, which they're pretty sure are the other couriers. All the Torquesan money will soon be recovered."

"What about the Leong brothers?" Frank wanted to know.

"They caught the Leongs at Honolulu airport. And guess where they were headed?" Nancy said.

"The Torquesas," Joe and Bess said together.

"You got it," Nancy said. She turned to her father. "Rachel really didn't know what Tanga was using her hotel for. But part of their agreement was that she do him a favor when the time was right, no questions asked. I guess you could call her an unwilling accomplice. Morita says he's pretty sure she won't go to jail and will get to

214

keep the hotel—if she can find a legal way to bail herself out."

Carson smiled sadly and gazed out at the surf.

George broke the awkward silence. "Hey, it's so nice out, why don't we hit the beach after I've finished eating your meals?"

Everyone laughed, and Nancy saw her father crack a smile, too. "Sounds good to me," she said, taking Carson's hand.

"But if I ever try to get on a surfboard again," Joe said, "somebody stop me please!"